4-EVER THEIRS

JAYNE RYLON

Sign Up For The Naughty News!
Contests, sneak peeks, appearance info, and more.
www.jaynerylon.com/newsletter

Shop
Autographed books, reading-themed apparel,
notebooks, totes, and more.
www.jaynerylon.com/shop

Contact Jayne
Email: contact@jaynerylon.com
Website: www.jaynerylon.com
Facebook: Facebook.com/JayneRylon
Twitter: @JayneRylon

OTHER BOOKS BY JAYNE RYLON

<u>DIVEMASTERS</u>
Going Down
Going Deep
Going Hard

<u>MEN IN BLUE</u>
Night is Darkest
Razor's Edge
Mistress's Master
Spread Your Wings
Wounded Hearts
Bound For You

<u>POWERTOOLS</u>
Kate's Crew
Morgan's Surprise
Kayla's Gift
Devon's Pair
Nailed to the Wall
Hammer it Home

<u>HOTRODS</u>
King Cobra
Mustang Sally
Super Nova
Rebel on the Run
Swinger Style
Barracuda's Heart

Touch of Amber
Long Time Coming

COMPASS BROTHERS
Northern Exposure
Southern Comfort
Eastern Ambitions
Western Ties

COMPASS GIRLS
Winter's Thaw
Hope Springs
Summer Fling
Falling Softly

PLAY DOCTOR
Dream Machine
Healing Touch

STANDALONES
4-Ever Theirs
Nice & Naughty
Where There's Smoke
Report For Booty

RACING FOR LOVE
Driven
Shifting Gears

RED LIGHT
Through My Window
Star

Can't Buy Love
Free For All

<u>PARANORMALS</u>
Picture Perfect
Reborn
<u>PICK YOUR PLEASURES</u>
Pick Your Pleasure
Pick Your Pleasure 2

DEDICATION

For everyone who supports my work by buying my books. I appreciate that you have kept me in the business of doing what I love this long, and I hope that never changes. Thank you!

CHAPTER ONE

"Stop. Stop. I'm going to pee my pants." Andi Miller gasped between bouts of hysterical laughter. She swiped tears from her cheeks as her three obnoxiously adorable roommates demonstrated their best attempts at twerking from various places around their kitchen. Sadly, Simon could definitely shake his ass better than she could. He put on quite a show from his perch atop their rickety table, threatening to turn it into kindling with sharp swings of his hips. The guy could easily have paid his portion of the rent and then some if he'd gotten a job as a go-go dancer.

"We're only trying to help." Cooper punched Simon in the leg then grappled him to the floor. If she didn't act fast, this could deteriorate into another of their infamous wrestling matches. The last one of those had resulted in the annihilation of a beanbag chair. She was *still* discovering tiny foam beads scattered throughout their apartment months later.

"I mean, it's not like you've come out of your room long enough to pick up any of our moves in the past four years, with all that studying you insisted on doing. You don't want to get embarrassed on the floor tonight, do you?" Reed asked as he simulated humping a cabinet.

Well, that wouldn't be a problem, seeing as she hadn't quite told them the truth about her destination for the evening. Dance club, hook-up spot—same difference, right?

Their over-protectiveness made her white lie necessary.

Besides, she owed them the same courtesy they showed her when it came to keeping their sex lives separate from their home lives.

The guys never brought women to the apartment. Or at least they hadn't in ages. Not since early in the first semester of their freshman year when one of their one-night stands—to this day, they wouldn't tell her which of them had slept with the poor girl—had tried to make herself some morning-after breakfast and ended up with a black eye courtesy of Andi's fist.

Hey, how was she supposed to have known it wasn't an intruder out there whipping up a frittata before absconding into the night with their meager college-grade possessions? Milk crate furniture might be hot on the black market for all Andi knew. If some of the oomph propelling her swing had actually been fueled by jealousy instead of fear, she'd hidden that pathetic fact as best she could from both herself and her roommates.

Ruining their friendships wasn't on her agenda. She wasn't the sort of girl who knew how to screw around then act like sex had been no big deal. Though she had chemistry with each of her roommates, how awkward would it have been to have followed through on it and slept with one of them?

Takeout and movie nights with the others would never have been the same.

Andi admitted it. She was sheltered as fuck. Though her vocabulary had gotten a hell of a lot more colorful as a result of her co-habbing with this trio of idiots for the past four years, she hadn't done a lot of exploring relationship-wise. After all, she spent most of her free time with Cooper, Reed and Simon. Who would approach her with those three hovering over her, snarling and baring their teeth at any guy who got too close?

God, she was going to miss them.

The thought of giving up their second-to-last Saturday night together had her rethinking her plans. Except this might be her last chance to eliminate her regrets about not having a single fling during her college experience. It would help round out her academic studies and the rewarding social experiment living with three dudes had turned out to be.

This was supposed to be her training ground for the real world.

Now that she'd accomplished the majority of her goals—by graduating at the top of her class and scoring a prime position in her field—maybe she could make some time to fill the emptiness growing inside her as she accepted that she'd be forging out on her own soon. The lack of a relationship hadn't bothered her so much when she'd had school and her roommates' friendship to occupy her.

All of that was changing.

So was she.

Andi wanted to be ready for what came next.

"Was it that good for you?" Simon flashed a wicked smile as he teased her.

"Huh?" She snapped herself out of her daze.

"Our dancing."

"Oh, yeah. Definitely. It was so hot I need to go take a shower." She rolled her eyes and giggled some more as she abandoned the kitchen for their shared bathroom. If she was sweating a little, it was surely from nerves over what she was about to do, not because they'd affected her.

Sure.

She scrubbed herself then spent a while drying and curling her hair before applying what dashes of makeup she owned—a bit of mascara and some nude lip gloss. The whole time, she kept wondering what tonight might be like if she could spend it with someone she knew and trusted instead of gambling on a blind date set up by her well-meaning chemistry lab partner.

Andi bit her lip then harrumphed and fixed the damage, at least mentally reminding herself not to rub her eyes before she could wreck them too. She sighed then rested her forehead on the door, praying for some direction. Was she making a mistake? Or would it be an even bigger one to pursue the foolish ideas tempting her to feel out her roommates about her proposition?

Before she could make up her mind, a rap on the door rattled her brains.

"Ouch. Fuck." She stumbled back.

"Yo, Andi. Quit hogging. I drank three beers with dinner, and I gotta piss," Reed groaned. "I forgot what it's like to wait on someone trying to be girly."

Aaaaaaaaand... That sealed the deal.

They were too much like brothers to ever see her as a woman. Which was exactly how she'd wanted things while they lived together. She grinned as she opened the door.

Reed squashed past her in the doorway, wedging them together when he froze. "Damn. Uh, you look...great."

"The magic of wearing something other than sweats and one of your roommates' old shirts *sans* a bra." She shrugged.

"I kind of prefer the no-bra part." Simon waggled his brows from where he scarfed another helping of now-cold pizza for second dinner.

When she turned to him with a smile, he paused mid-bite.

"What?" Andi finger-combed her hair as she stepped from the bathroom so Reed could relieve himself in peace. Not that the guys didn't invade her privacy often when she was in the shower, or vice versa. The trials of a single bathroom for four people had absolutely played a part in her collegiate years.

"I told you," Reed shouted through the door.

"They're right. You're hot." Cooper took her hand and spun her around. "I'm not sure we should let you go out like this, young lady."

"Whatever, Dad." She chuckled until he finished twirling her, though it hadn't entirely been a joke. With her parents both gone, these guys had stepped up and filled a huge, painful void as best they could. They were, and always would be, her family.

In the heels Andi had borrowed, she was closer to Cooper's height. Meeting his warm stare, she caught the spark of something serious there.

Could he actually be attracted to her?

She knew each of them appealed to her in various ways—Cooper's gentlemanliness and tact, Simon's playfulness and daring, Reed's sense of responsibility and control.

As if a sliver of possibility was the only prompt her subconscious required, she blurted the thoughts that had been haunting her for the past hour. Okay, longer than that. At least since she'd agreed to this outing. Probably since the day she co-signed their lease.

"Maybe you guys should come out too?" She prided herself on the fact that she only stammered a little when she said, "Or I could stay home and we could have a private party instead."

Simon blinked at her, the pizza still lodged half-inside his mouth.

Cooper's fingers tightened around hers. His other hand landed at her waist to steady her. But he didn't say anything.

The door opening behind her broke the moment, forcing them apart.

Reed emerged as the toilet finished flushing in the background. It was as if her silly dreams circled the bowl then vanished down their clanky pipes when he grimaced. "What's that? Don't back out now. You've been looking forward to tonight all week. It's about time you cut loose. On your own. You've earned this."

"Oh. Okay." If they noticed the tremble in her faux smile, they didn't call her on it.

Andi decided to quit fucking around. Playing a game where she didn't know the rules was a sure way to lose. Reed was right. She had to learn to stand on her own, without leaning on them. Because in a matter of days, they wouldn't be part of her everyday existence anymore.

Graduation was a week away.

Her new life, the one where she'd be a lab tech in a prestigious pharmaceutical research firm—one that didn't include her roommates—was calling.

"Go ahead. Have fun," Simon said around a mouthful of pepperoni. "Besides, we've already—"

Cooper cleared his throat, but it was too late. She realized they must have dates. Of course they did.

"Hey, you'll be fine," he promised. He looked away before adding, "You don't need us."

Andi swallowed around the lump in her throat. She took a step forward and then another before grabbing her wristlet and keys out of the bowl at the end of the countertop. If she was going to do this, she couldn't linger. Otherwise, she'd never convince herself to leave.

"Be safe!" Reed shouted as she closed the door softly behind her, determined not to let the stinging of her eyes turn into real tears and screw up her mascara.

CHAPTER TWO

ndi tugged the fitted skirt of her stretchy lace dress past mid-thigh, watching her bare skin peek through the intricate patterns. Her outfit was modest enough to seem like a nun's habit compared to the latex corsets or fishnets and boy shorts she saw others wearing. Still, discomfort for the women whose breasts spilled from their necklines rubbed off on her.

It wasn't that she was a prude. At least she didn't think so, but she'd never had the freedom to put herself out there like that. Or someone to admire her and support her inner sex kitten like the men escorting their dates to the discrete doors of Flesh, a local sex club, seemed to be doing.

She was out of her league. Totally intimidated.

Crazy to have considered this a reasonable first step on her foray into hook-up experimentation.

She hadn't even made it across the parking lot from her ancient Civic to the dark building, which looked too innocuous to be the den of iniquity it was purported to be, before she was second-guessing herself. And that was *precisely* why she had to keep going.

Andi steeled her spine and lifted her chin, hoping the few assets she had were at least displayed to their best advantage when she perfected her posture. A simple kind of woman, she went with what she knew best. Directness.

"Good evening," she said to the man monitoring the entryway before he could address her.

"It is." He smiled sincerely at her greeting, making her wonder if she might not seem as out of place as she felt. Until he asked, "Can I see your membership card?"

"Oh. Um. I'm not..." She shrugged. "I'm meeting someone here."

The guy's lips dipped into a frown. "Let me check the guest roster..."

"Not necessary," a newcomer said as he approached at a jog. Tall and fit, he filled out his jeans and lightweight sweater in a way that made her hum softly. Hopefully to herself. "You're Andi, right?"

"Yes." She beamed up at him, relieved she wouldn't have to suffer the mortification of being turned away or the discomfort of waiting for her date in some holding room. Her propensity for arriving early had never landed her in trouble before. *Note to self: Be fashionably late to dates from now on.*

See, she was learning shit already.

As smoothly as one of her roommates might, her blind date leaned down and kissed her cheek before placing a possessive hand on her lower back. Immediately, she felt something inside her unravel. She might not have any clue about what she was doing here, but her lab partner—Veronica—seemed to have done her justice by fixing Andi up with her brother.

During a study session, Andi had confided that she was thinking of sneaking in a night at Flesh before her time in town ran out, hoping Veronica would be her wing-girl for the outing. Instead, her friend did one better. Turned out her brother was a member. Grossed out as Veronica was about believing he even *had* a sex life, she figured it was safer to play matchmaker than to let Andi take a spin in random-partner-roulette.

She had to agree.

Cross one thing off her list of possible disasters for the evening. This blind date was definitely not a hardship to look at. Or socially inept. He brushed his thumb over her spine casually, making her shiver. In response, he drew her tighter to his side. So far, definitely good. Soooo good.

"Nice to see you again—"

Her date talked over the bouncer's greeting. "Let me take care of this real quick, grab us a couple drinks, and we can get to know each other."

The guy working the door seemed kind of irritated at this point. She glanced over her shoulder, but there wasn't anyone waiting. It wasn't like they were holding up a line or anything.

Andi would be glad to move past him before he could change his mind about allowing her admission.

Her date refused to allow her to cover her portion of the entry fees, then asked if she wanted to store her things in one of the club's secure lockers. Veronica had outlined Flesh's basic policies. Cell phones weren't allowed in the playrooms. Better to take care of that now than have to put the brakes on later and introduce any additional awkwardness into the situation.

"Sure." She smiled and kept up their small talk as he walked her through the rest of what she needed to know. Maybe this hadn't been such a bad idea after all. With a shy smile, she glanced up at him. "I'm sorry, I didn't catch your name before. It's Peter, right?"

"Huh? Oh, yeah. Shit. I kind of forgot my manners when I saw you out there." He cracked a smile that dazzled her. "It's a pleasure to meet you. Seriously. I was kind of worried about how well my sister knew my type."

He lifted her hand and dusted a kiss over her knuckles.

Andi wasn't the sort of woman who fished for compliments. It still made her grin when he added, "My sister will be getting a kickass graduation present after this, that's for sure."

"You don't think it's weird?" She cleared her throat and tried not to blush. "You know, that I wanted to…"

"Nah. No judgment here, honey." His grin turned sort of wolfish at that. "I *am* a member here. And you saved me the trouble of hunting down someone half as interesting as you to play with tonight. I'm happy to give you what you're looking for."

To her horror, Andi felt her eyes prickling again. This guy was being a perfect gentleman. He was cute, and easy to talk to, and didn't seem to judge her. So why did she still wish she was at home?

"What if I can't—?" She swallowed hard.

"Hey, hey." He tugged her into a light hug. "No pressure. First time jitters. Everyone gets 'em. Why don't we go out there and dance? See what happens? I promise, you'll be relaxed in no time."

"Thank you." She squeezed his waist, noticing that he smelled nice, if different than the guys she was used to. "I appreciate you being so cool about this."

"Come on." He interlaced their fingers then led her to the main area. "How's a fruity cocktail sound?"

She was more of a beer girl, really, but she'd already been enough of a pain in his ass. "Great."

He winked at her then showed her to the edge of the dance floor before shouting, "Wait here. The bar's always mobbed on the weekends. I don't want you to get crushed."

Andi nodded, grateful for a moment to compose herself. Then she watched as her date waded through sensual bodies pulsing with the music. It did take a while for him to make his way to the front of the line. Eventually, he took something from his pocket along with his wallet as he paid for their booze. She angled her head for a closer look. An overzealous dancer bounced into her, jostling her.

"Sorry!" The guy grinned as he braced her until she was steady.

"No problem." She smiled back.

"Meeting new men already, huh?" Peter returned, swishing the neon-pink umbrella through her drink a few times before handing it over. "I know I won't be lucky enough to keep you for long."

She laughed before taking a sip, then another, of the sweet concoction. "This is delicious. I can't taste the alcohol with all this stuff in here."

"I think that's the point." He smiled then tucked her against him as he swayed in time to the beat that began to reverberate through her the more she imbibed.

By the time her straw sucked pure air, she was already feeling looser. Warmer too, though Peter's thigh pressed between hers as they settled into the rhythm might have had something to do with that. She was in capable hands with him.

"Come on, let's dance for a bit." He set her empty glass on a tray at the edge of the room along with his own. Then he tugged her onto the floor and showed that his hip action was nearly as good as Simon's. She might have forgotten to breathe for a bit since the room seemed to spin. Or maybe that was anticipation along with a solid buzz.

Either way, she couldn't say she minded the sensation much.

By the time Peter's hands began to wander up her thighs, below the hem of her skirt, she had started peeking around for the entrance to the lower level and the temptations she'd heard about. The impressive bulge rubbing her ass when she spun her back to his front and let him lead her through the song didn't hurt either.

He dipped his head and took her earlobe between his teeth, making her tremble when he asked, "Ready for more?"

Without bothering to speak, she nodded.

"Good girl, Andi," he crooned before escorting her from the floor.

The band of his arm around her waist was welcome. It kept her upright and moving toward the experience she'd been hoping to have tonight despite the extra wobble in her knees. Probably from arousal—didn't all her romance books describe it as causing weak knees?—along with that drink he'd treated her to. It had been a strong motherfucker, that was for sure.

She was sticking to beer next time.

Andi shook her head to clear it some as they navigated a set of curving stairs to the level below. When she slipped, Peter caught her, sweeping her into his arms.

A riot of giggles escaped her parted lips. She clung to his neck, hoping he wouldn't notice how blitzed she was and turn her away. Willing herself to sober up, she concentrated on the feel of his flexing muscles beneath her cheek.

Until he ruined the moment by muttering under his breath, "Ah fuck, I might have given you too much..."

Too much?

As if he'd plunged her into a pool of ice water, every ounce of her flirty excitement vanished.

Too much what, exactly?

Immediately, the chemical formula of a half-dozen date rape drugs sprang to mind. Or at least they would have if her brain cells had functioned properly. Alcohol wasn't the culprit here, though when mixed with whatever else he'd given her, it could amplify the effects. Oh fuck, she was in trouble.

"You drugged my drink?" Andi cringed as her accusation slurred. She wished she could slap him. Her hand felt as if it were forged from steel where it dangled by her side. So did her tongue, for that matter.

Sound assaulted her ears in garbled waves.

"It'll help you relax. That's all, honey. Don't worry. This is what you want, remember?" Then why was his hand over her mouth, threatening to suffocate her even as it prevented her from shouting out. "You'll thank me tomorrow."

No, she would fucking not!

Andi fought. He'd crossed every single one of her lines. The entire point of this night was supposed to be about claiming independence. Taking control of her sexuality on *her* terms. Not on someone else's or at the whims of some chemical reaction.

"Shhh…" he warned as he ducked into a private room and bolted the door. Without breaking a sweat, he subdued her revolt. Thrashing brought bile to her throat, weakening her further.

Slumping in his hold, Andi realized too late that there was nothing she could do to stop what was about to turn her night of discovery into one that would haunt her for the rest of her life.

Peter dropped her onto a relatively soft surface, maybe a bed. She couldn't focus enough to tell.

A tear tracked down her face as he ripped her panties.

"Don't cry. I'm still going to make it good for you. I swear." His promises didn't reassure her in the least. Because this couldn't possibly be further from the dreams she'd had of what tonight would be like. "Give it a minute. You'll be into it again. Calm down."

When another tear fell, he shook her, hard. The jostling rattled her teeth and caused her to bite her tongue. The iron tang of blood filled her mouth.

"Stop being dramatic. You're going to like this. Let me show you."

Did he really believe that bullshit?

Andi wished she had enough control to hammer him in the balls. Despite repeated attempts, her limbs did nothing more than flop around as he manhandled her. Gathering the last of her willpower, she focused on making her throat work. A scream escaped. Or at least she hoped she hadn't simply imagined the desperate sound. "Help!"

Then only flashes passed before her eyes as she struggled to keep them open and failed.

Peter's face contorted in rage. His fist zooming toward her.

A crash in the distance.

"Andi!"

Wishful thinking made her imagine she heard her roommates answer her silent prayers. The idea of them nearby brought her a shred of comfort right before she blacked out.

CHAPTER THREE

Reed sat at the bar, rattling the remnants of the ice cubes in his glass. Shitty whiskey seared a few layers of cells from the inside of his esophagus. It couldn't touch the chill in his chest from their near miss with Andi.

He'd seen the look in Cooper's eyes as he'd emerged from their bathroom earlier.

They'd made it this long without fucking up. Making a mistake now, with a single week left until graduation, would be unforgiveable. But *damn* how he'd wanted to do the wrong thing for once in his life.

Andi wasn't theirs. No matter how much they'd wished she could have been over the past four years. Soon she wouldn't even be their roommate. Their constant torture. Their daily reminder that there might never be a more perfect woman for them to share. One who happened to be completely off-limits too.

Fuck.

Simon had been right. They needed to get laid tonight. Badly.

With finals and work study they hadn't had time to blow off steam lately. So they'd agreed to treat themselves to a reward of sorts. A night out at Flesh, the one place in town where their reputation was an asset instead of a hindrance.

Already they'd been approached by no less than a half-dozen women eager to try out their legendary brand of passion. Unfortunately, none of them seemed to appeal to the guys. Hell, he didn't give a shit who they picked. They would never be the one woman he wanted, so he always went for whatever piqued Cooper and Simon's interest for a night.

A couple of nicely stacked women in sparkly g-strings hopped onto the bar to give them a better view of their offering. The only thing he could think of was finding glitter clinging to his dick in the shower later. It would piss him off that he'd settled for someone so vastly different than Andi.

Again.

Reed swallowed. It was getting harder to do this.

What would happen when he couldn't stick with Cooper and Simon anymore?

Would they go on without him?

Would their bond be broken?

He wasn't sure he could stand to lose them too.

Prepared to get his head in the game and perform like they expected him to, he cracked his knuckles.

"Oh, great. Are you in a shitty mood?" someone familiar asked as he crashed onto the stool beside him. "Because I don't need any more drama tonight."

Reed smiled despite himself. "Hey, Peter, what's up?"

The guy grunted, ordered a couple of doubles then dropped his head in his hands as if trying to keep his brains between his ears while he waited for the alcohol to start flowing. Reed could relate.

Cooper leaned in from Reed's other side. He couldn't resist teasing the guy. "Can't find anyone to play with or what?"

"Sort of, I guess. But worse." He shrugged as Simon got up and walked over to stand behind Reed and Peter for the whole story. "I was supposed to be meeting this chick my sister set me up with. Kind of a pity date thing. Probably for the best we didn't meet up. It would have been a guaranteed lay, but boring as hell, I'm sure. Still, Veronica is going to be *pissed*. She really likes this girl and wanted me to kind of look out for her, you know? Nobody can hold a grudge like my sister, and I need to borrow her truck to move out next week. That's probably not gonna happen now."

"Well, did you check with Micah at the door? Or is she a complete no-show?" Reed wondered. "Can't be held against you if she chickened out."

"That's just it." He scrunched his eyes closed for a moment then slammed the first drink the bartender set in front of him. "She's here somewhere. Micah let her in with her goddamned date."

"I don't get it," Simon interrupted. "I thought that was supposed to be *you*?"

"Here's the part Veronica's going to have my balls over." He downed the second shot then cleared his throat. "I was at a friend's earlier today. We were smoking weed. I was high and bragged to some other dude who was hanging out about coming over here tonight to meet her..."

Reed groaned. What an idiot! "And he scooped her out from under you."

Peter hung his head. "Yeah, I think so. I passed around the picture and note from my sister. They know everything I do about her. Ah, well. Hopefully they're having a helluva time and my sister will never figure out it wasn't actually me who boned her. The only thing that's kinda bugging me—"

"What?" Reed's eyes narrowed. If it wasn't that some young girl was getting fucked by a stranger who was lying to her, what *would* trip his faulty conscience?

"Well, the guy we were toking with..." He grimaced then looked over at Reed with dread in his eyes. "I think he sells Mind Erasers sometimes."

"*Roofies*?" Simon nearly lunged over Reed's back as he snarled. He'd never hurt a woman, or stand for someone else to do it either.

"You're a fucking dumbass, Pete." Cooper cursed. "What's this girl look like? Maybe we saw her."

"She's kind of natural and sweet. Dark hair past her shoulders, straight. No fake orange tan bullshit either. Nice full lips, curvy...about this tall." He held his hand at just the spot Andi had looked up at Reed from earlier, after she'd dolled herself up for her bold night out. "I was sort of looking forward to something different. Shit. My sister's gonna kill me. They're chemistry lab partners."

Warning bells went off in Reed's head. His stare whipped to Simon's then Cooper's. Their faces were downright ghostly.

"What's her name?" Simon barked before he could.

"Andi. With an *I* even. How cute is that shit?"

"Jesus. Peter, tell the manager. Put security on it. Now!" Reed stood up fast enough he knocked the stool to the ground, scattering dancers around them. Cooper leapt to his feet. Already standing, Simon had a lead of a few paces on them. He was a fast fucker when he needed to be. And he didn't hesitate for a moment.

They would have gone on a seek-and-destroy mission to stop this guy even if they didn't know the woman he was likely about to abuse, but...*Andi.* No! They had to find her.

Fast.

Waiting for the authorities wasn't an option.

Who knew what that asshole would do to her? She didn't belong in a place like this. Could be taken advantage of so easily. Why hadn't she told them the truth about what she was doing tonight?

Because they would have acted like barbarians, of course. Prohibited her from going.

At least she would have been safe, if furious. Her anger he could handle, the alternative...he could not. *Would* not.

"Andi!" he shouted, though no one heard him above the blaring music. He hauled his phone from his jeans and poked her picture in his contact list. It went straight to voicemail.

They blew through the main floor as if by some unspoken agreement. If she was still up there, dancing, the bouncers could deal with the situation. But if she'd already gone down below...

Reed ran faster.

He cleared the three flights of stairs to the underground playrooms with a leap for each one. "Split up!"

He bolted through a corridor they'd strolled along together on numerous other occasions, much more pleasant ones, while Connor and Simon searched others. He thought of all the things they'd done together in the shadowy corners of the club and couldn't imagine how someone would enjoy taking instead of giving to their partner here.

Breaking plenty of rules, which would get him banned from Flesh for life, he interrupted more than one couple in the middle of a delicate situation. The cell phone in his pocket was another violation. He didn't give a shit. It might be necessary to call for help when he found Andi. *When*. No matter how many rooms he barged into, they weren't the right ones.

Shit! Were they too late?

Had the creep taken Andi somewhere else instead?

Behind him, Cooper and Simon were causing just as much of a ruckus as he had.

With only a few more areas to clear, a shriek rent the air. "Help!"

His heart stopped.

"Andi!" Reed skipped ahead to the source of the scream. He bashed the door with his shoulder, ignoring the pain that radiated along his arm when the solid wood shuddered but didn't cave. He backed up then kicked, this time splintering a section. Another smash of his boot blasted it wide open.

And there she was, unconscious, at the mercy of some date-raping scum. He called to his roommates, "Over here, guys!"

Simultaneously, his fingers curled into a fist.

"Hey, what are you doing? This is a private—"

The bastard never finished his sentence. It would have been hard to minus the teeth Reed popped from his too-pretty face, knocking him out cold in the process.

He didn't waste any effort on pummeling the guy. There'd be plenty of time for punishment later, after they'd made sure Andi was okay.

She was his first priority.

Now and always.

Simon and Cooper raced into the room, shouting curses when they took in the rivulet of blood trickling over her cheek and the ripped underwear dangling from a corner of the bed.

If this fuckwad had raped her, he wouldn't live.

Reed roared, but wouldn't be distracted from his primary goal.

Afraid to touch her with so much rage storming through him, he looked to Cooper, who rushed to Andi and gathered her in his arms. He leaned down and allowed her breath to dust his cheek before gently touching the pulse point in her neck. Satisfied, he tried to rouse her. "Sweetheart, are you okay?"

He shook her softly, trying to bring her around with encouraging nonsense as Simon trotted into the hall to flag down a staff member. The call for medical assistance came shortly after.

Reed's heart slammed so hard in his chest, he was afraid it might crack a rib. He'd never been so scared in his entire life as he was at that moment. When he returned, Simon didn't crowd Andi. Instead, he came to stand by Reed, putting a hand lightly on his forearm.

"We've got her. No one's going to hurt her anymore."

"Damn straight, they're not," he rasped, barely reining in the urge to kick the shithead on the floor.

Whatever it took to keep her safe, they would do it.

Cooper looked over at them and nodded softly, as though he could hear Reed's thoughts.

Then it was chaos. He found himself blocking a crowd from flooding the room, stealing the last of Andi's privacy. Unmovable, he kept everyone out until the EMTs arrived a few minutes later.

Reed, Cooper and Simon watched as they worked on Andi, stabilizing her.

"She's lucky you got here when you did," the first responder admitted in a conspiratorial whisper. "It doesn't look like he'd raped her yet. The drugs will clear out of her system by themselves in twenty-four hours or so. It wasn't a dangerous dose. Well, other than..."

"Yeah. Thanks." It was all he could manage.

Reed stood by the gurney as they prepared to wheel Andi out to the waiting ambulance. He clasped her hand tight. Maybe too tight since her eyes fluttered open.

"Hey," he murmured. "You're going to be okay."

Just then a woman approached. "Reed?"

He couldn't remember her name, but he hadn't forgotten how it felt to be buried in her ass while Cooper fucked her pussy and Simon fed her his cock. Not exactly something he felt comfortable reliving with Andi there, wounded. "I heard what happened. I'm so sorry."

"Not now." He dismissed her without ever looking away from Andi.

Cooper and Simon flanked him, keeping the woman at a safe distance. But he'd hurt her feelings, something he prided himself on never doing with the women they enjoyed together. It was a personal low for him, and she got caught in the crossfire.

"Cut him some slack, please?" Cooper tried to reverse the damage Reed had done. "Andi is special to us."

"Unlike me, who was just some random lay you three shared? I was wrong about you guys. You're like all the rest. Total assholes," she snipped before marching away, justifiably offended by their callous disregard when she'd only been trying to be kind.

Reed couldn't find it in him to care. He still stared at Andi.

Which was how he knew she'd heard exactly what the woman had said. Her eyes grew wide. She sucked in several rapid, ragged breaths through the oxygen mask covering her mouth.

Her busted lip moved as though she tried to speak, but he hushed her.

"Later. We can talk about it at home. When you're better," he promised, though he admitted to himself he was banking on the drugs lingering in her system to erase her memory.

Andi nodded, a tiny bob of her head before her eyelids drooped again.

Cooper rounded the gurney and clasped her other hand in his. "We've got you, sweetheart. You're safe now. Don't worry about anything else."

Her gaze roamed until it landed on Simon.

With all three of them surrounding her, she relaxed.

"Time to go," one of the medics told them.

Andi tensed.

"I'm staying with her," Reed insisted. "We live together."

"Fine. But you're the only one." The EMT began to wheel her away, cutting off their opportunity to argue.

"We'll meet you there after we talk to the cops," Cooper called as Simon blew Andi kisses.

Reed held her hand the whole way to the hospital, even after she'd succumbed to unconsciousness once more.

He wasn't sure he could let go ever again.

That could be a major problem.

CHAPTER FOUR

Andi plucked fuzz off the well-worn comforter that cocooned her like a friendly hug. Snuggled into her nest on her slightly saggy mattress in the apartment she'd grown to love, she already felt better. It beat the cold, crisp sheets and too-firm hospital bed she'd been confined to for the previous day and a half, hands down. Although she'd spent most of her time in the hospital knocked out, it had been a fitful sleep.

On her own turf, she could pretend that the whole Flesh incident had been an awful nightmare. Except that Reed, Cooper and Simon had avoided her since they'd brought her home the night before. They'd deposited her in here, fed her some soup, then disappeared. Where were they?

Lying there debating how long she could hold off before having to pee, she heard the door crack open. "Hello?"

"Hey, Andi," Reed whispered, as if afraid he'd hurt her by speaking full volume. "Sorry. Was just checking in on you since you don't usually sleep so late."

"Had a rough couple of days." Her joke fell flat.

Reed grimaced. "Yeah, I noticed. I shouldn't be bugging you." He turned to go.

"Wait." Andi sat up, gathering the covers to her chest like a shield. What did he think of her and the things she'd done? Was this awkward tension ever going to fade?

She supposed it would when she moved out next weekend.

Andi sighed.

"Hey, you okay?" Reed ambled closer.

She patted the bed beside her hip. "I'll be better if you'll come here and talk to me for a while instead of acting like I caught a major case of the cooties in that club."

Thankfully the tests they'd run at the hospital had confirmed that wasn't the case. But if the guys had been a few minutes later...who knew what might have happened? Andi shivered.

"You cold?" he asked, sinking beside her. His solid bulk caused the mattress to dip and she rested against his side. Though he stiffened, he didn't shove her away, so she made herself comfortable.

"No." Especially not with him to heat her up. "Jumpy, that's all."

"Ah, shit." He put his arm around her shoulders and squeezed her tight. "I've got you, Andi."

She didn't mean to say it out loud, but she did. "Only for a few more days. Then I'll be on my own. Alone."

"Hey. That guy isn't gonna go anywhere near you ever again," Reed promised. "He's going to have to answer to the law for what he did. And after that..."

"Don't do anything to get yourself in trouble. I'm fine. No one got hurt." She patted his abdomen, noting how tense he was. The cut of his six-pack was clearly defined beneath his soft T-shirt.

"I beg to differ." The fingers of his free hand traced over her lips more tenderly than she knew he was capable of. The puffiness had subsided some, but her mouth still felt weirdly overstuffed. Getting decked had that effect, she supposed.

"Okay, well, it could have been a lot worse." She sighed and nuzzled his chest, curling up against him as naturally as if she'd been made to fit there.

It surprised her when a growl bubbled up from his chest and he half-shouted, "Andi, what were you thinking?"

She blinked a few times, caught off guard by his sudden outburst. Had he been bottling up his frustration with her, waiting for her to recover before unleashing it?

Before she could respond, Simon and Cooper rushed into the room like a pair of guard dogs. Cooper slid onto the opposite side of her bed and tugged her away from Reed. She didn't mind the loss of her comforter when he wrapped his arms around her protectively. She couldn't help but burrow into his hold. "Hey. I thought we agreed not to harass her."

"Seriously, Reed. What the fuck?" Simon climbed onto the foot of the bed and rested his palm on her shin. His thumb rubbed arcs below her knee.

"Sorry." He scrubbed his hands over his face, which was when she noticed his bruised and scabbed knuckles.

"Reed!" She would have flown to him, but Cooper's arms held her tight. "Your fingers—"

"Are fine." A wave of them dismissed her concern. "Trust me. I'd have gladly traded a few broken ones for a dent in that fucker's face. I didn't get the chance to make a real impression before the cops showed up, though."

"Thank God," she sighed. She couldn't stand the thought of him embroiled in legal problems because of her.

"You give a shit what happens to that monster?" He looked at her like she was nuts.

"No. But I care a lot about what happens to you, dumbass. Especially over something that was my fault." Her shoulders slumped in Cooper's hold.

"Hey, that's not fair." He kissed the crown of her head lightly. "You aren't responsible for that bastard drugging you. You know, he wasn't even the guy you were supposed to meet there."

"He wasn't?" She sat up straighter.

"Nah. We know Peter. He's a dumb fuck who doesn't know when to keep his mouth shut, but he's not evil. He wouldn't do that," Simon told her before explaining the mix-up. It was the first time they opened up about that night. "We saw him up at the bar. He told us what was going on and we put two and two together..."

Andi closed her eyes for a moment, relieved. Knowing it wasn't Veronica's brother that tried to harm her somehow made her feel less stupid. She'd trusted her friend, and allowed that faith to cloud her judgment when it came to some of the shady things that imposter-Peter had done.

She thought about how he'd cut the bouncer off before he could be greeted by name, how he had never referred to Veronica as anything other than "my sister", and the glimpses she'd caught of him tampering her drink. Those clues made so much more sense in hindsight. They alleviated the majority of her self-recriminations. Maybe she'd be ready to talk to the police and give her statement this afternoon.

The guys had held them off while she recovered.

"Can I ask...and you don't have to tell us if you don't want to..." Reed trailed off, very unlike him to seem so unsure.

"No more secrets," she swore. "It didn't work out so well the last time I tried that."

"Ah, sweetheart." Cooper rocked her lightly.

"Okay." Reed nodded. "What were you looking for at Flesh? It's not like you—"

"How would you know what's *like me* when it comes to sex? Son of a bitch, how would *I*?" She hated the sting of tears that sprang up in her eyes in a flash. This was exactly why she'd resorted to something so out of character. The fear that she might not ever find out these things about herself. A huge piece of her was missing because she'd neglected to excavate it and had instead buried it deeper within herself.

If she was honest, it was partly the fault of these men, her roommates. She'd never wanted to betray them or the profound feelings she had for them. Partly, she was to blame, because she'd never had the guts to be honest about that. With them or herself.

That was going to change now.

She had nothing more to lose.

They only had days left together either way. After graduation, she was moving a couple states away for her lab tech job and they were not. Reed had a business plan to execute, Cooper was enrolled in law school and Simon—a sports medicine major—had been recruited to continue the work he'd begun with the college's football team during his internship.

The three guys were going to stay together, probably find another roommate. Some new girl to replace her with. Maybe one who wouldn't be too stupid to take a chance and tell them how she felt about them.

Fuck. It was now or never.

With the threat of looming awkwardness removed, she laid herself bare to them. "Look, I'm just going to say this. I probably should have gotten it out of the way a long time ago, but...I didn't want things to get weird."

"What are you talking about, Andi?" Simon asked, his hold on her leg growing stronger.

"I know I acted like I didn't bother to date because I was busy studying." This was harder than she'd imagined. Shit. She powered through without pausing or she might never finish what she'd started. "That's not true. Not entirely. I just...never found anyone that interested me as much as you guys do. Then all of a sudden I was about to graduate and I freaked, thinking about what I'd missed out on the past few years. I wanted to do something wild for once before it was too late. Even though it wasn't what I really needed, I figured it'd be good enough to keep me from regretting all the things I never did with you three. I was wrong."

There, she'd said it.

Her confession hung in the air between them like a giant stinky fart.

None of them recoiled, or jumped her, or even seemed to breathe. They were killing her.

"So, now that you know that embarrassing factoid, I won't be upset if you want to pretend to be real busy for the rest of the week until I'm out of your hair." She cleared her throat. "Or if you want, I can pack up and get out of here early. My apartment in Cunningham is ready any time."

"You're not going *anywhere*," Reed practically snarled.

Andi flinched.

"Don't be scared. He's not angry," Cooper murmured to her. "He's trying to keep himself in control."

"Huh?" She peeked up at him.

"Yeah, I'm pretty sure we'll be jerking off to that speech for the next twenty years." Simon laughed softly. "Considering we've talked about what it would be like to sleep with you more often than we've fought over which team deserves to win the World Series."

Wow, that *was* a lot.

"Seriously?" She tried not to squeak, and failed miserably.

Reed nodded. He stared at her with an intensity she'd never seen fully unveiled before. It didn't frighten her in the least. It was sexy, and alluring. Uh-oh, this was bad. Or awesome...

"Then why didn't you do anything about it?" She looked at each of them for a few seconds, trying to discern the answer in their carefully blank features. "I'm not an idiot, you know. I heard what that woman said to you at Flesh. And I've been thinking... The frittata girl. The reason you wouldn't tell me which one of you slept with her wasn't because you were being chivalrous, it was because you *all* fucked her. Together. Didn't you?"

"Umm, yeah," Simon caved. "That was the first time. We were drunk and she sort of looked like you with beer goggles on."

"Now I'm glad I hit that lucky bitch," Andi grumbled, not giving a shit if it made her petty.

Reed burst out laughing. It was nice to see him unwind a little. "You're crazy, you know that?"

"That's why you love me." She hadn't meant it like it sounded. There was no way to take it back, though.

"Yep, it's one reason." He huffed out a sardonic sigh. "Andi, don't you see? We thought it was better to keep this part of us away from you. Your friendship means too much to us to fuck it up with sex."

"And I'm telling you that I'm not some judgmental cow. It pisses me off that you didn't trust me enough to show me who you really were." She would have put her hands on her hips if Cooper wasn't practically smothering her in his trembling arms. "In fact, your kink turns me on. And I've already said that I'm attracted to all of you. Therefore..."

"No." Reed crossed his arms.

"What's the problem here?" Andi wondered.

"Other than the fact that you nearly got raped two nights ago?" Reed had definitely not mastered subtlety.

"Yes, other than that." She cleared her throat. "What some random piece of shit did to me has no bearing on how I feel about you three. I trust you.

Completely. That's sort of the point. I probably *won't* be comfortable setting up an online dating profile or taking home some cute guy from a bar for a very long time. So this is it for me. My last chance to try this out in a safe environment before giving it a go for real. I think it will actually help, you know?"

Cooper hugged her tight. Instead of making her feel trapped, his arms surrounded her in protection. It was all the proof she needed for her theory.

"Okay." Reed groaned. "Two other things. First, I admit it. I'm a selfish bastard. I've never been jealous of these guys before when we've played around with a woman. I guess because they didn't matter like you do. I don't mean that in a dickhead way. I respect every person we've ever been with. But it was exclusively about a good time. Something simple. They were onboard. They knew we weren't looking for more than to rock their world for a single night. With you...I don't know if I *can* share without causing permanent harm to one of them."

"If it's all the same to you, Andi..." Simon winced. "I like my balls attached."

She laughed.

"I'm also worried that you're not ready," Cooper said softly. "It's intense, having sex this way. What if it's more than you can handle?"

"There's only one way to find out," she insisted. "Come on, be my outrageous college experiment."

It hurt her to imply that her interest in them was only skin-deep. But she wasn't sure they'd go for it any other way.

No, no, that was the old her talking.

She quickly added, "Okay, that's not really what I mean. Hiding how I felt didn't work out before and I don't want to screw up again."

She swallowed then dug deeper, exposing her vulnerability to them and trusting them not to eviscerate her. Deep down, she knew they never could do that. "Let me be with men I trust and care for. No strangers. Either now, or later, that's what's going to happen. I'm curious and turned on. Don't make me go somewhere else to find out what it's like to give in to these urges."

"Andi—" Reed's mouth pinched at the corners. He still wasn't convinced.

She drew a deep breath, prepared to persuade him that he wouldn't be responsible if it turned out she couldn't handle going from zero to sixty in her race to embrace her sexuality.

"Actually," Simon spoke up, surprising her with the quickness of his compromise. Had he thought of this before? "We don't have to throw her straight into the deep end."

"What do you mean?" Reed asked him.

"Why can't we each have a night alone with her?" As usual, he seemed to speak without considering the consequences. The most impulsive of their quartet, his instinctive calls were either brilliant or disastrous. No telling which this would be. "Build up her experience, introduce her to what we're like in bed as individuals. Give her a chance to change her mind if it's too much. If she can handle each of us separately, then...at the end of the week, we'll spend our last night together."

"Sounds like one hell of a graduation present," Andi whispered, trying not to bawl when she added, "And a perfect way to say goodbye."

"Ah, fuck," Reed cursed.

Cooper clung tighter to her while Simon gave her a look she could imagine belonging to a kicked puppy. None of them persisted in their futile objections. Could they need this as badly as she did?

"Good. So who's first?" She couldn't help but lick her lips as she looked at each of them.

"Cooper," Reed and Simon said simultaneously.

"Why me?" He grunted when she smacked his chest. "I mean, not that I'm complaining..."

"Because you've got the most manners. You'll take things slow. Do it right," Reed explained, and Simon nodded.

"I should say no." He looked down at Andi with a rueful smile. "But I can't. I've wanted this for a long, long time."

"Me too," she admitted.

"Take the rest of today to get back on your feet, longer if you want it," Reed ordered. "Now that finals are done, you have a whole week to relax. Tomorrow or the next day is plenty soon enough to blow our friendship all to hell."

Andi nodded, and their course was set.

When she felt up to it, they escorted her to the police station. As she strode from the building, her story told, she felt calmer. Ready to put it behind her. They spent the evening watching moves, playing video games, eating takeout and generally being normal, as if each of them feared the end had come sooner than they'd bargained for.

After this, nothing would be the same again.

Andi couldn't decide if she should mourn or rejoice over the change. She supposed that depended on what happened in the next few days.

Holy shit.

CHAPTER FIVE

Andi did a double take at the list in her hand. She'd made it all the way to aisle seven before she realized what she was truly doing.

After waking around lunchtime, her head still shaking off the last of the fuzzy feeling from her drugging, she had found herself alone in their apartment. Like she had every Tuesday after classes since they'd moved in together, she'd grabbed the top sheet of paper off the magnetic notepad stuck to the front of their refrigerator then headed out to shop for groceries.

When she got home, she'd give the receipt to Reed. At the end of the month, he'd deduct the guys' share of the food from what she owed in rent. They ate so damn much, sometimes she got a refund. Usually, her cart overflowed with frozen pizzas, beer, boxed mac and cheese, and an assortment of similar junk food.

Today, it contained—judging by the price—a nice bottle of wine, two steaks, a bag of fingerling potatoes and some bittersweet chocolate squares. Each of those items had been added in Cooper's impressive script.

She didn't mind shopping for her own romantic dinner with him in the least.

In fact, she'd bet he'd realized that collecting the items he'd carefully thought about and placed on the list to facilitate his seduction would heighten her anticipation.

Score one for him.

Not that she could stand to be much more excited about their date night.

Rushing through the rest of the chore, she wondered if he'd be waiting for her when she returned. Or maybe she'd have some time to borrow another dress from the ladies next door and curl her hair. He'd seemed to like what she'd done with it last weekend.

Why hadn't they done this sooner?

She tried not to regret the terror she could have avoided if they had.

Through it all, she worried. How would she make sure it was good for him too?

Tonight shouldn't be exclusively about her. She wanted to leave them with amazing memories of her. If she was totally honest, she'd admit she felt the need to brand each of them with some piece of her so that they could never forget what they'd shared. Not only this week, but also in the past four years.

As she'd suspected, she hadn't even made it to the cracked concrete stairs at the end of their sidewalk before Cooper came out to meet her. His long legs made short work of the distance between them. Tall and lankier than their other two roommates, he was a pleasure to watch in motion. His chestnut hair had a bit of a curl to it. The shaggy cut framed his classic features nicely too.

"Hey," he said by way of greeting.

She was too busy ogling him—now that she could do so with open interest—to protest when he insisted on taking every one of the plastic bags overflowing her fists from her instead of sharing the load. Typical.

"Find everything you needed?" he asked with a charming smirk.

"I think so. Except for the jumbo condom assortment. You might be out of luck." She couldn't resist torturing him.

"Seriously?" He stopped dead, as though he might sprint to the nearest drugstore without bothering to set down their dinner first.

"No, of course not." Andi laughed. "But you should see the look on your face. Relax, Cooper. Even if there were a sudden latex shortage, you could spend the night teaching me how to give killer BJs instead."

"Oh God." He groaned. "This is going to be tougher than I thought."

"To be with me? Like that?" She swallowed hard, wondering if she could keep herself from crying like a sore loser if he backed out now.

He shook his head and glared at her, something he rarely did. "To make it until after dinner before fucking you senseless."

Good thing she wasn't carrying anything or she would have dropped it right there. The electric shocks his promise sent through her zapped her heart.

"Hey, I'm fine with some countertop action. Getting messy in the chocolate. You know, whatever works." She tried to play it casual and failed miserably. Because the reality was, she was dying for something to take the edge off her need. A taste of what was to come.

"As delicious as that sounds..." His resolve seemed to be cracking for a moment, until he shook his head. "Nope. We're doing this the right way. Come on, help me figure out how to bake something edible for dessert."

"Only if you'll let me eat it in bed." Andi tried not to pout.

"Deal." He grinned.

They worked together seamlessly in the kitchen, him searching for recipes while she got out the rest of the ingredients they'd require. As much as she hated to admit it, being with him like this relaxed her. It was just another night hanging out with Cooper.

Except with the lights turned low and a mismatched pair of candles burning on the kitchen table, it was impossible to deny that this evening would have the ending she'd often wished it would.

When they'd set the table and the last item was down to five minutes remaining in the oven, Cooper surprised her. He came up behind her and rested his hands on her hips, pulling her back to his front so that there was no denying his arousal.

Maybe by *jumbo condom assortment*, he'd actually been referring to the size of each condom, not the quantity in the box. Hmmm.

Automatically, she tipped her head to the side and exposed her neck. He didn't disappoint, leaning down to kiss her there. Shivers exploded along every nerve ending in a four-inch radius. It was so easy, and so addictive. She wanted more.

"You're certain?" he whispered. "This is what you want?"

"Yes," she gasped as she rocked backward against him.

Instead of pulling her closer, he set her away. When she spun toward him, a muscle in his jaw ticked. "Go get dressed for dinner then. I left you something on your bed. Wear it if you like it. Or don't if you'd rather not. I love you like this, Andi. In your comfy clothes with your hair wrapped up in that clip like you always have it. I only thought you might want to try something different, that's all. Maybe it's time each of us grow up, just a little. Become who we're meant to be someday."

She could see it then, him wearing the hell out of a designer suit, arguing high-profile cases. In the not too distant future, Cooper would be a man of power and wealth. One who would back up his gentleman tendencies with a suave flair no woman could resist.

For him, and herself, she would do this. See if she could be the kind of woman he would need.

Andi darted into her room and gasped when she spotted the dusky-purple silk wraparound dress set out with stockings, a crocheted wrap and matching heels. Sure, they were basic, practical, but she loved them and could see wearing them often. He hadn't tried to make her into some slutty version of herself, but a more sophisticated one instead.

She hoped she could live up to his vision of her.

For a few minutes, she sat on the edge of her bed, fingering the lush fabrics.

"How'd I do?" he asked from the doorway, his voice husky.

"Amazing." When she looked up, her eyes widened. She had been talking about his selections but the word certainly fit the man before her now. He'd cleaned himself up, put on a black button-down shirt and a new, pressed pair of slacks. The fact that he'd left the sleeves unbuttoned, rolled up on his forearms, and hadn't bothered with socks or shoes somehow only heightened his attractiveness.

"Damn, Cooper." She fanned herself.

"Mind if I watch?" he asked with a jerk of his chin toward her pretty dress.

At first nervous, she grew bolder when she whipped her T-shirt over her head then shimmied out of her yoga pants. Standing before him in a basic black bra and panty set, she wished she had something fancier to tempt him with.

He didn't seem to mind in the least, jamming his hands in his pockets as if to keep from reaching for her.

Knowing she could affect him, even a little, was all the encouragement she needed.

Andi smiled as she started with the stockings, rolling them up her calves as she savored the caress of the fine material on her freshly shaved legs. Next, she stepped into the shoes.

Cooper groaned. "You could stop right there and I'd be happy."

"Wouldn't want to risk burning myself with dinner." She winked.

"Then you'd better hurry up and get that dress on." His composure fractured, just a bit.

Andi loved it.

She did as he instructed, though, letting the garment fall into place with a swish around her knees. When she looked in the mirror across the room, she was proud of herself and the way she looked. Not super model material, sure. But for an average woman, she rocked his dress and the newfound confidence his appraisal inspired.

"You're gorgeous, Andi." He came closer and wrapped his hand around the back of her neck, angling her face upward.

Before either of them could think too much about the boundaries they were crossing, he swooped down and kissed her. It was long enough, sensual enough, and satisfying enough to curl her toes and make her forget about dinner in favor of a different sort of hunger entirely.

Except right then the smoke alarm went off.

"Son of a bitch!" he shouted, and tore into the kitchen.

Andi laughed, her heart full of joy. She admired his goofy grin as he rescued their dinner before it sustained too much damage. Just a little extra sear on the edges.

Together, they ate. They talked and laughed and shared comfortable silences.

When she pushed her plate aside, he stood and stalked to her place at the table.

Andi rose, going all the way to her tiptoes so that she could wrap her arms around his neck and pull him toward her for another taste of his smile. This time he didn't bother keeping things between them polite.

CHAPTER SIX

Cooper nudged Andi's lips with his own until she parted them and granted his tongue entrance to her mouth. When she wobbled as a result of the onslaught of pleasure he triggered, he put his hands on her ass. Nothing timid about the firm squeeze of his long fingers, either. Without further encouragement, she hopped then wrapped her legs around his waist, thrilled when he began to walk her down the hall toward her room, never once breaking their connection or pausing their kiss.

He kicked her door closed then crossed to her bed in a couple long strides.

The care he took when setting her gently onto the bed made her blink rapidly.

"You okay?" he asked between butterfly kisses at the corner of her mouth. "I can go slower. Or stop."

"No, no. Please don't." She writhed beneath him, trying to increase contact with his torso despite the slight separation he'd put between them. "I'm fine. Just...touched. You didn't have to make our evening so romantic. I wasn't expecting that, but I'm glad you did. It's nice to know this means something to you too."

"You have no idea, Andi." He sank his fingers into her hair and settled over her, aligning their bodies as he continued to drive her wild with his mouth. He was by far the best kisser she'd ever had the pleasure of making out with. Not that she had a huge sample size to compare to, but enough—she was sure—to be certain of his skill.

She figured the same would be true of his fucking.

Andi had slept with her date to the senior prom, how cliché, and a couple of other guys the summer in between high school and college. None of them had done much for her. It hadn't seemed like a sacrifice to abstain while she focused on her grades and her eventual career.

Now she realized how damn much she'd been missing out on.

Cooper trailed his fingers along her arms, making her moan shamelessly as her spine arched, pressing her body deeper into his hold. He swiped the shawl from her then got to work untying the ribbon at her waist, which kept the dress he'd selected for her closed.

He unwrapped her as carefully as he had the simple presents she, Reed, and Simon had given him for birthdays and Christmases throughout the years. Savoring the moment. Never rushing. Endearing him to her with his gratitude and appreciation for the homemade gifts.

Nothing was different today.

Reverent, he praised her as he revealed more of her skin to his awed petting. "Your skin is so soft, Andi. So pretty. I'm afraid of touching you, messing you up."

"You could never do that," she promised, returning the favor by cupping his cheek in her palm then reaching beneath his collar to stroke his upper back. She couldn't wait to have him fully nude. His gorgeous form on display. "You're not going to hurt me, Cooper."

How she wished that wasn't a lie.

Her heart would never make it through the next week unscathed. It was a price she was willing to pay to have him, and their other roommates, even if only for the next one hundred and twenty-five hours or so. There'd be plenty of time later to count the cost to her soul.

His warm breath puffed over her as he sighed between nibbles at her neck. Eventually he wandered to her collarbones and finally across the swells of her breasts, lavishing attention on each square inch of her that his mouth traversed.

Cooper reached beneath her, lifting her so that he could ease the dress off the bed and drape it carefully over the nightstand. Then he returned, unfastening her bra and peeling it off of her to unveil her breasts to his searing gaze.

Andi couldn't say what made her do it, but she plumped the mounds, cupping them and arching her back, offering her assets to him.

"Yes," he hissed before descending. His talented suckling combined with flicks of his tongue to prove she'd made the right choice.

Her heels drummed on the bed as he drove her crazy even before his hands wandered south to the edge of her panties. It took everything in her to wheeze, "Wait, please."

Cooper stopped, immediately. So different than her horrific experience a few nights ago. He waited for her to elaborate or simply to leave. Whatever she decided, he would respect her wishes. It was incredible, the sense of empowerment he gave her. Being with him, like this, made her feel as though she could rule the world.

Or at least direct their rapture.

She'd settle for that.

"If you put your hands in my panties, I'm going to lose my mind." She smiled shyly up at him. "Before you do that, could you get undressed? I want to see you too. Feel you against me, skin on skin."

"Hell yes." He knelt between her knees and began to unbutton his shirt. "When you talk like that, you make me so fucking hard, Andi."

"I noticed." She grinned at the thick bulge in his pants. "You could skip to the good part, you know. I won't be offended if you hurry."

"It's all the good part. Being with you like this is more than I could have dreamed. And I thought about it a ton." His eyes sort of glazed over for a moment, and she believed him. Damn. It made her feel better about the numerous times she'd woken to dreams of one or all of her roommates spending their evenings on the couch in an entirely different way.

He shook his head then smiled down at her. "Besides, Reed will kick my ass if I don't treat you the way you deserve."

Andi laughed at that, though she could see the kernel of truth in his eyes. She was so screwed.

How would she leave them behind?

How could she not?

Her future lay elsewhere and they all knew it.

Cooper tore his shirt open, causing the final few buttons to fly across the room and *tink* off the window. "Oops."

She grinned as he made equally fast work of shedding his pants and his gray briefs, leaving himself completely open to her unfettered appraisal. He was even more amazing than she'd guessed. All of him was lean and tight, well-muscled but balanced. And his cock...

Andi swiped her knuckles across her lips, hoping she hadn't actually drooled.

"Better?" he asked with a self-assured grin.

"Yep. Definitely prime beefcake." She chuckled at his mock-offence.

"Hey. I'm a man, not some slab of meat. I've got feelings and shit, you know." He couldn't even finish that with a straight face. "I like the way you look at me, sweetheart. Feel free to do it anytime. Makes a guy feel pretty damn good about himself."

"You should." Opening her arms, she reached them up to him. "Now come back. I miss you."

Her throat squeezed as she realized how true those words would be soon.

He lowered himself over her again, this time making her cry out when the weight of his erection thumped onto her belly and their bodies aligned as if they'd joined them a million times before. "I don't know what I'm going to do without you."

"Don't think about it now. Let's just enjoy," she begged. There was no other way she'd make it through tonight or the others to come.

"I intend to." He kissed her more deeply then, with a sense of urgency he had masked before.

She was right there with him.

And when they broke apart, gulping for air, he slithered down her body. He levered his shoulders between her legs, then peeled her panties over her hips.

Andi raised her legs and helped, kicking the scrap of cotton into the corner somewhere before splaying her legs on either side of his torso. Without a moment's hesitation, he buried his face in her pussy, devouring her with a ferociousness he hadn't come close to when he'd consumed his dinner earlier.

He murmured to her about how good she tasted and how wet she was between laps of his tongue and the tricks his mouth played on her clit. Her entire body began to vibrate before long.

"You close, Andi?" he asked as his fingertip circled the entrance to her body.

"Yeah." It was all she could manage.

"I want to watch you come for me. I'm going to put my fingers inside you—you ready?" he double-checked, probably because of everything that had happened recently.

"If you don't, I'm going to—"

She never did get to finish that thought. Because the steady pressure of him invading her clenching sheath combined with the lingual Olympics he played over her clit had her shattering on his face.

Andi climaxed with unabashed enjoyment. She didn't try to tone down her reactions or hide how fucking much he pleased her. Rapture blew through every molecule of her body. Just when she thought she couldn't feel any better, he redoubled his efforts, taking her higher and drawing out her passion.

He might have continued going down on her for hours if she hadn't gotten his attention with a tug on his riotous hair.

He looked up without pausing the action of his tongue. The erotic sight was too much. She lost it again in another mini-peak.

Andi could have sworn she felt him laughing against her moist folds. Damn him.

As she shuddered, she ground out the only four words that mattered. "Fuck me. Now. *Please*."

It was the last one that seemed to do him in.

His eyes melted into golden pools that shocked her with their brilliance.

At the same time, he reached to the nightstand and the box of condoms he'd set there before. She'd hardly started to catch her breath before he had a packet open and was rolling the thin rubber over his impressive length.

Next time—if there was one—she swore she'd return the favor and blow him. It would be fun to grant him as much pleasure as he had given her.

For now, she could only think about fusing them together. Taking him inside her body and making them one, at least for right now. Not for one instant did fear enter the equation. Sure, he was huge compared to the guys she'd been with, but he'd never harm her.

She knew that down to her bones.

So she spread her legs wider to make room for his hips and glanced between them to watch as he fit the fat head of his cock to the opening of her pussy. He'd guaranteed she was wet enough to take him easily. In fact, he slid across her sensitive flesh a few times before he found the optimal angle to penetrate the tight ring of muscles at her entrance.

Nudge by nudge, he prodded her open and began to sink inside.

Andi's stare flew to his, which had never left her face. They locked together gaze to gaze and cock to pussy. Nothing had ever felt so right to her.

"Perfect," he whispered. "I knew you would be."

He drilled deeper within her until they fused completely. When she held every inch of him, he paused as though as overwhelmed as she was.

"Want to make it good—" He gritted his teeth and looked up at the ceiling.

"You already have." She put her hands on his chest and kneaded the muscles there. "Don't hold back. Not now, Cooper. We don't have time for that."

Deep lines marred his face as he realized that what she said was true. They were gone quickly, though, as he refocused on what they did have. Now. And it was glorious.

With a worshipful streak of curses, he began to stroke, dragging his cock over the most amazing spots inside her. Every time he triggered a clench of her pussy, he fucked harder, faster, dooming them both to the inevitable end of their lovemaking.

Through it all, though, he was gentle. Liquid and smooth. Never jarring.

He treated her as though she was precious, and his deference touched a spot deep in her core that his body alone could never reach.

"Coop—" she tried to warn him, but she couldn't.

She didn't need to since he was right there, living the moment with her.

"Yeah. Me too." He kissed her hard as he pumped into her again and again. Full of him and the glow he surrounded her with, she surrendered.

Andi shattered around him, hoping the rhythmic pulses of her body were enough to milk him dry. His primal shout, along with the slightly jerky pumps of his hips that accompanied him filling the condom with jet after jet of his come, guaranteed it was.

When the storm of passion had blown over, neither of them moved.

A pervasive calm stole over her. Content, she wallowed in his weight and warmth as their hammering hearts eventually returned to normal. It was no secret that Cooper was an expert-level snuggler. She often cuddled with him on the couch of their living room while watching TV.

This was different, though.

Cooper rolled to his back. He wrapped his arms around her and shuddered before breathing deeply with his face buried in her hair. His genuine caring and the honesty of his physical intimacy with her were evident in his hugs. What neither of them had the words to say, they showed each other with tender caresses and lingering touches.

For a long time, they wallowed in the bliss they'd manufactured together.

Eventually, Cooper left her—though only for a minute—when he retrieved their chocolate cake.

As promised, he fed it to her in bed, letting her lick icing from the spoon and then from his body when she decided she was hungry enough for seconds. And thirds. And fourths.

It was nearly dawn when they fell into a very sated sugar coma together.

Andi was sad, though not surprised, to find his place by her side empty when she woke just before lunchtime the next day.

CHAPTER SEVEN

"Happy hump day, Andi." Simon grinned as she stumbled into the kitchen with only a T-shirt on. It was one of the guys', though she had no idea who she'd swiped it from when she'd gone fishing in the laundry basket they shared. That was Cooper's contribution to the household and she didn't feel guilty in the slightest about letting him take care of the chore.

"Same to you," she responded. For a moment, she wondered if he was commenting on her just-fucked look, the day of the week, or the fact that it was his turn today, but then she decided any of the above were funny.

A giggle forced its way past any potential embarrassment threatening to stifle it. Maybe that had been his intention. She studied him as he flitted around their kitchen, grabbing a mug and dumping a bunch of sugar in it, just like she liked.

A few inches shorter than Cooper, he was bulkier. All that time hanging around the jocks had influenced him some. He burned off his constant supply of energy in the gym most days and trained along with many of his patients.

Strong and capable, he never failed to impress her.

"Thanks," she murmured as she wrapped her fingers around the steaming coffee he brought to her at the table. Haze gradually lifted from her mind as she neared the bottom of the brew. Then she looked around, fully awake for the first time and wondered, "Where is everyone?"

"Cooper's at a meeting with his guidance counselor, setting up his classes for next semester and shit. Reed's meeting with a couple of investors." He grew serious for a moment, something that didn't sit well on his jovial shoulders. "They're not planning on coming home today. Didn't want to intrude. I can call them if you'd rather they didn't stay away. Cooper especially..."

Andi wouldn't deny that she missed him already, but neither would she make Simon feel like he was any less important to her. She wouldn't have agreed to this arrangement if that were the case.

"What did he tell you about last night?" she asked. She had no idea what the rules of this new game were.

"That it was the best of his life." Simon smiled. "I'm happy for you, both of you. Glad that it rocked. I won't stand in your way if you want more of that."

"Of course I do," she admitted.

His face fell for a split second before he smiled, then kissed her on the forehead. "Let me give him a call."

"Hey, that's not what I meant." She snagged Simon's hand and drew him back. "I regret not doing this sooner. When we had more time. Is it weird for you, knowing that I slept with him last night?"

"I wouldn't say that." He shrugged. "It's a lot of pressure, though, to live up to the matching set of shit-eating grins you're both sporting this morning."

It shouldn't have made her heart race to know that she'd pleased their friend, but it did.

"You know me. I don't like to think too much about stuff. Overanalyze it. I leave that to Reed and Cooper." Simon winked at her. "All this *communicating* is stressing me out. I like to jump right in to doing."

Andi had Cooper to thank for boosting her self-esteem enough to suggest, "Well, if you want to..."

She grabbed the hem of her shirt and began to walk it up her thighs suggestively.

"Christ. Not now." He slapped his hands over his eyes.

The violent reaction might have offended her if his arousal wasn't apparent given the thin cotton of his shorts. She laughed.

"If you do that, we'll never leave the house. I want to spend some time with you." He cleared his throat. "Aside from all this sex stuff, it really is our final chance to hang. I want to say goodbye properly."

Just like that, he had her poised on the verge of tears.

"Don't you dare. If you crack, I will too." He hoisted her from the chair and spun her so that she faced her room. "Go get ready. Wear sneakers and clothes you can move in. I want to take you to the gorges."

"Hiking?" She nodded and clapped. It'd been a while since they'd made time to roam around the woods together.

"Stop bouncing until you put a bra on or no one's going anywhere," he teased her before snapping a damp hand towel at her and barking, "Hurry up. Some of us didn't sleep half the day away."

She heard him loading the dishwasher as she took a record-breaking shower then threw on some clothes. It hadn't really occurred to her before how they split the household tasks around here. They'd each picked up some slack, making life easier for everyone in the process. Andi would be giving up more than she had realized when she drove off on Sunday.

Staring into the mirror, she wondered for the first time if she was doing the right thing.

"Annnnnnnndiiiiiiiiiiiiiiii," Simon whined, obviously out of whatever tiny portion of patience he had started with. "I'm bored."

She swallowed hard and ran out to meet him. It was impossible not to smile when his contagious enthusiasm spread to her. They held hands as he drove them to one of their favorite parks. She kept his grip the entire time they walked along the rocky path.

The burning in her thighs felt good, refreshing. It also gave her a sense of control over her body. Whether it was on purpose or not, her roommates knew how to make her feel strong, even when she wasn't sure that she was.

As they hiked, Simon told her dumb jokes, sang songs and generally kept her entertained every second. She didn't once have time to ruminate on what she'd done the night before or debate if what she was about to do was wise. Or fair. Or crass.

Playful and adventurous, Simon had always ensured their lives were full of impetuous fun.

This day was no exception.

It was impossible not to enjoy herself. And him. Especially him.

They wound their way along canyons and stopped to admire waterfalls before he helped her cross the stream on a series of logs and rocks. Never once did she feel off balance when he clasped her hand in his, leading her through what seemed like his personal playground.

Along the way, they stopped to investigate anything that caught their interest, and once to enjoy some of the snacks he'd stashed in his backpack on an informal picnic.

She hadn't realized quite how far they'd gone when they reached one of the lookout points on the trail. Standing with him at her back and his arms looped casually around her waist, she rested the crown of her head on his shoulder.

Together they drew in the crisp mountain air.

They might have stayed for a while before heading back down from the zenith except that a storm cloud chose right then to roll over from the opposite side of the peak.

A booming clap of thunder was followed by an instantaneous downpour.

Simon cursed as he tugged her into one of the shelters on the side of the path. It resembled a campus bus stop. A Plexiglas roof and walls provided an unobstructed view and a place to take a break from the wind at the summit on the metal mesh bench beneath.

"Let me guess, you didn't check the weather report this morning?" She grinned, sure of the answer before she'd asked.

"Don't expect miracles, babe. Just 'cause I'm finally going to get to sleep with you doesn't mean I got any smarter last night." He pinched the bridge of his nose. "Shit, Andi. I'm sorry. I didn't mean to ruin…"

"You didn't." She stopped him right there with the only thing she knew for certain would work.

Andi went onto her tiptoes and braced her hands on his shoulders. When he looked down at her, she ambushed him, covering his mouth with hers.

He tasted like salt and summer.

They kissed as thunder rumbled in the distance and the rush of rain beating the leaves surrounded them. Steam rose off the rocks where the hot earth met the cool water, blending and becoming something ideal.

She understood exactly how that felt.

When Simon drew away, blinking down at her with slumberous eyes, she knew what to do. Listening to her instincts, she toed off her shoes, tucked her socks inside them, then quickly dispatched her shirt and pants, folding them neatly on top of her sneakers.

Finally, she unhooked her bra then wiggled out of her panties, ensuring she'd have some dry clothes for the ride home.

"Come on, Simon. Play in the rain with me?" She curled her finger suggestively at him as she stepped out into the downpour. Her hair was plastered to her skull in no more than a few seconds.

The water coursing down her face, breasts and torso felt divine. Invigorating and sort of taboo, like her liaisons with her roommates. It was a sensation she could easily get obsessed with.

Twirling around with her arms outstretched, she laughed as she caught the rain in her palms.

Until she heard him say, "You're the most beautiful thing I've ever seen in my life. Insane, but gorgeous."

And then he was there—naked as she was— kissing her, drawing her down onto the soft grass.

CHAPTER EIGHT

The truth of it was Andi would never have done something so outrageous if it wasn't for Simon's impulsive influence. He—and each of the guys—brought out a side of her that didn't exist without them. They enhanced her experiences, and made her a more well-rounded person.

She wondered what she gave them in return.

Simon peered down at her, rain dripping from his nose as he paused to study her soaking features. Grinning up at him like a fool, she hoped he liked what he saw.

He pressed her arms above her head and held her wrists in one of his broad hands. With her immobile, he began to feast on her. He started with her eyelids, kissing each, before moving on to the tip of her nose.

Spending an inordinate amount of time on her lips and tongue, he nearly caused her to lose track of where they were. All she could feel was him and what he did to her.

When his free hand covered her breast, the diamond-hard tip threatened to dent his palm.

"Too cold?" he asked.

"Not anymore." She smiled up at him when he adjusted his position above her to blanket as much of her exposed skin as possible.

Andi expected to see steam rising off his sculpted ass like it had those boulders a few minutes ago. She couldn't help but ogle his ripped frame. Heat poured off him, keeping her toasty as he continued to lap rainwater from her skin.

When the ground began to turn to mud, he said, "You don't belong in the dirt, babe."

Releasing her wrists, he put his hands on her waist. Before she could ask what he meant, he'd rolled, pulling her over him with her knees straddling his narrow hips.

Suddenly, it was her turn to investigate the wonders of his body. The entire time she allowed her fingers to tease and prod his firm muscles, roaming the landscape of his build, the rest of her picked up on the subtle shift of his pelvis that accompanied the flexing of his ass and thighs in response to her handiwork.

Soon she was grinding against him, sliding along the length of his bare cock. Thicker than Cooper, he might have been a little shorter, but nothing she could complain about in that department.

Damn. If he felt half as good inside her, she was likely to fly right off this mountain when she came. There was no doubt now that she would. They'd gone too far to turn back before taking each other over the edge.

"Andi, hang on," he grunted loud enough for her to hear over the white noise made by the rain spattering around them and the periodic base of the thunder. His hand flailed on the grass beside them, searching...

She spotted the foil packet a few inches from his fingers and plucked it from the tangle of wildflowers it had fallen in. Ripping it open with her teeth, she allowed herself to embrace her feral side, and the naturalness of the act they were about to share.

Not one ounce of hesitation or embarrassment had room to squeeze past the joy he inspired in her heart. She couldn't wait to share this with him. Their first time, maybe the last too...

"Don't go too fast," he cautioned when she winced, mistaking the pleasurable pinch of his fat head spreading her pussy wide for the twinge in her chest.

His hands were on her hips, supporting her and keeping her from impaling herself. Gradually, they introduced his shaft to her channel. Empty and aching, all she wanted was to be full. Of him, of life, of happiness, and pleasure.

Though it might have been an unconventional variety, their entire day together had been foreplay of sorts. Waiting another moment to be joined completely wasn't in either of their best interests.

So she took charge, swatting his hands from her and leaning forward. This time her fingers latched around his wrists, turning the tables. Though he could have broken her hold, he didn't, humoring her.

The twitch of his cock within her insisted that he didn't mind much.

"I love seeing you like this." He groaned her name into the wind. "Fierce and sure. Take me, Andi. Take whatever the hell you want."

Something wild came over her then, allowing her to do exactly as he had given her permission to do. She pushed back, embedding him deeper within her on every rock of her hips. It thrilled her that he rose up from below to help, to meet her halfway and make her desires a reality.

She shook her head from side to side, relishing the stings imparted by the wet clumps of her hair, which whipped her shoulders.

Andi felt like some tempest goddess called down from the heavens to thrill this mortal man.

Her laughter might have frightened someone else. Simon seemed awed by her transformation from bookworm to deity. He urged her to fuck him harder.

So she did.

When finally she held all of him within her, they called out simultaneously.

Her clit rubbed against the muscles at the base of his shaft, making her eyes nearly cross. Her pussy clamped on him, hugging him solidly. The motion of her fucking switched from bobbing over him to some kind of figure-eight grind.

"Is that good for you?" she asked.

When he groaned and banged his head on the soft ground beneath it, she figured that was decent enough confirmation.

Andi concentrated on squeezing him tight as she lifted off a bit. Then she eased up as she pressed close once more. When she could hardly concentrate on anything but the mounting pleasure, she released his hands.

Eager, he directed them to her brightest pleasure points in a flurry of motion that would have made a champion boxer envious.

All the while, as she used him for her own pleasure, his hands flew over her from her breasts to her ass. Finally, one of them wormed between their bodies to manipulate her clit.

Resisting that additional stimulation would have been impossible.

"I'm not going to last much longer, Andi." He groaned. "Come, please. Come on my dick."

Flying with him was the most alluring prospect of all.

As if on command, her body obeyed his desires. She went rigid, her body bowing as the pressure built to impossible proportions within her.

"Yes! Yes!" he shouted to the sky.

And she knew it was because she'd given him what he needed.

Andi came so hard, she worried she might break his cock. Through her entire orgasm, he pumped into her, fucking her like mad when she lost the strength to do it herself. She held on tight to his broad shoulders and rode the waves of ecstasy for as long as she could.

As they lay there, her half-collapsed over Simon, who had crashed—completely blissed out—in the mud, the rain began to relent. It dialed back from downpour to drizzle, then a fine mist, and finally quit entirely.

They sighed in unison as birds began to sing once more and the sun peeked through the clouds, chasing away any lingering chill.

When his cock softened enough to slip from her body, she whimpered. It was a long walk back to the car, yet the only thing she wanted to do was settle in right there. Her scuffed knees and tired muscles proved she wasn't immortal after all. Damn.

"Got a little carried away there, huh?" Simon grinned as he levered himself to his elbows.

He cradled her against his chest as he climbed gracefully to his feet, carrying her to the shelter.

"Maybe just a tad." She giggled as she curled around him, hugging him tight. "It was worth it, though."

"Shit, yes, it was." He set her on the bench then snagged his shirt off the ground, using it as a towel to dry the majority of the droplets and mini mud puddles from her skin. As for himself, he shook off like a dog then stepped into his pants. He tried not to wrinkle his nose at the soggy mess his feet made in his sneakers.

Andi followed his lead, letting him assist her in getting trail-ready once more.

Just before they headed back, she drew him to the edge for one last view of the world far below. As they stood there, fingers linked, a glorious rainbow stretched in a perfect arc over the horizon. She couldn't help but think it was some kind of sign.

But what was it trying to tell her?

That this guy was *the* guy?

That nowhere was going to be better than here?

That something even more amazing was waiting at the other end of the rainbow?

More confused than ever, she followed him down the mountain. When they arrived at the trailhead, Simon turned to her, for once somber.

"You know, this wasn't what I had in mind for today, but you proved to me that the best things in life are always the ones that come as a surprise." Simon hugged her tight then tucked her into the passenger seat of his car.

They weren't quiet on the ride home. No, they sang along to the radio and passed each other an imaginary microphone for the good parts.

By the time they pulled into the driveway, her ribs ached from laughing.

Dirty and starting to shiver from the combination of her damp hair and the air-conditioning, Andi shouted, "Race you to the shower!"

They tore along the sidewalk then bounded up the squeaky wooden stairs of their porch. She shed clothes in each room between the front door and the bathroom.

By the time they were locked inside together, she wasn't sure she was going to need the balmy spray of their shower to get warmed up. Simon was looking at her like *that* again.

Sure enough, by the time he'd finished soaping her up, he had her bent over, palms on the tiled walls as he pounded into her from behind.

"What is it about fucking me in the water that you like so much?" he asked between labored breaths.

She laughed. Right there in the middle of a moment so intense she wouldn't have imagined it possible the day before. "I'm not sure. Quit chatting and finish the job. Then we can dry off and compare what it's like to screw in a nice comfy bed."

"Somehow I think I like this better." He put his foot on the edge of the tub for additional leverage and drove deeper within her.

By the time they finally crawled into bed together, neither of them had the energy to test out their theory. Besides, there was something about their carefree mating that simply wouldn't be the same in bright lights and ideal conditions.

Instead, Simon seemed happy to comb the snarls from her hair and put her back together, help her prepare for her reentry into civilization following their walk on the wild side. After he finished untangling her hair, he braided it then nudged her to her stomach.

A decadent massage relaxed her muscles, which were surprisingly sore—either from their trek or the sexual gymnastics she'd been undertaking. After all, he was an expert, trained in keeping athletes at their peak performance. His hands felt divine. But when she offered the repay the favor, he declined.

"Can I just hold you for a while, babe?" he asked.

For a guy usually so committed to motion and activity, it struck her as a deeply affectionate gesture. Maybe *this* is what she brought him, the ability to be calm—still in both mind and body—for once.

Andi cuddled against his side. She dropped a kiss over his heart, nuzzled her cheek on his shoulder, then embraced him every bit as tightly as he did her.

It was a long time before they drifted off together.

CHAPTER NINE

Waking up to a lonely bed was even harder the second time.

Andi rubbed her chest, hoping it was just a lingering sore muscle and not something less curable—like a slowly breaking heart—that was causing the ache there. No such luck. Despite Simon's magic hands and the amazing rubdown he'd given her before bed, she winced as she stretched.

She wasn't used to all that...activity.

Glancing at the clock, she was surprised to see she'd slept until noon again. This was the first time she'd been able to catch up on her sleep in years, so maybe it made sense. Committed to the decadence of the next few days before being thrust into the real world, she refused to be sorry about it.

After another quick shower, which loosened her some, she wandered into the kitchen. She smiled when she opened the refrigerator and found a plate with half a sandwich inside. There was a note on top, taped to the plastic wrap.

I know you like my leftovers. Just like Reed. HA HA HA -xoxo Simon.

Any other guy might have gotten smacked for that, but he didn't intend any malice. Especially after yesterday, since he'd probably filled his quota of *serious* for an entire decade. The chuckle he gifted her with helped ease her nerves a bit too. She owed him for that.

Speaking of Reed, by the time she was down to the crust of the bread and picking at the last of the good stuff from inside, he came through the back door with his hands covered in grease and an endearing smudge across his cheekbone.

Despite her recent overindulgence, her entire system purred at the sight of him.

In between both Simon and Cooper in terms of height and build, her inner Goldilocks declared him *just right.* His hair was darker than the others, nearly black, and his contrasting eyes granted him a shocking stare. They fluctuated between gunmetal gray and cornflower blue, depending on what he wore and the lighting in the room, not that she'd spent a disproportionate amount of time studying them over the years. Right.

Despite his calloused hands, he was a thinker—a strategist and a coordinator. Those traits were going to make his medical supply 3D printing start-up a smashing success. She couldn't wait to see him rising to the top and knew it wouldn't take long for him to get there.

Driven and focused, he wouldn't settle for anything else.

Engrossed in studying him, she didn't hear what he said to her when he noticed her sitting at the table.

"Hmm?" she asked.

"Don't act like you don't know what I'm talking about." He didn't turn to face her as he scrubbed his hands in the sink. "When were you going to mention that your oil light came on again?"

Oh. That.

"Never." She shrugged. "I'm gonna have to learn to take care of this shit on my own, right?"

"Not yet." He practically spit the words. "And you know we're not going anywhere. If you need help, we're not *that* far away."

"You're going to drive four hours to work on my car?" She didn't mean to be a bitch, but she also couldn't allow him to make false promises. The only way this was going to work was if she made a clean break when she walked away.

"I would if you'd let me." He shook his head as he dried his hands. "Sorry. I don't want to waste our time arguing."

"Me either." She came up behind him and hugged him, resting her head between his shoulders.

Reed put his fingers over hers then squeezed. "It's harder than I thought, and I knew it was going to suck donkey dick."

"I know." She sniffled, trying not to ruin the day with tears.

Then he turned in her arms and took her cheeks in his palm. "No matter what, don't forget how proud I am of you. All of us are. You deserve this job, this chance to make a difference in your field. It's a big deal. You're doing the right thing."

It felt natural to strain upward until he kissed her.

The first brush of his lips over hers felt like coming home. Ironic, since it was kind of the opposite. Andi committed the moment to memory and knew she'd think of it often when she got homesick. Hopefully his encouragement would give her the strength to stay the course on the long, lonely nights when she waffled over her decisions.

And she knew she would.

But he was right.

This was what she'd been working for. It was what she wanted.

Making a difference in people's lives, helping relieve the anguish of thousands of people… Well, she'd seen how both of her parents had suffered through long illnesses before finally succumbing. It was the best thing she could think to do with her life to try to prevent others from going through the same thing.

If she got really lucky, maybe some of her involvement in trials would lead to cures.

People like her wouldn't be so alone if their loved ones could be saved.

Any personal discomfort she might sustain had nothing on the upside. She had to do this.

Reed separated them and smiled at her. "You're going to make a difference. I'm just a selfish bastard, that's all."

She bit her lip and nodded once, because part of her was just as egocentric and pissed at what she had to forgo. Hard decisions, but ones she'd already made. And she wouldn't change her mind.

He wandered away from her then rested against the wall, closing his eyes to gather his thoughts or maybe just to keep her from scrutinizing those glorious eyes of his, which told her so much he never would say out loud. "Do you mind if we stay in today, Andi?"

"Not at all. Honestly, I'm still kind of recuperating from yesterday's jungle adventure." She stretched as she admitted it.

"I told Simon to be careful with you." His brows drew together, making his eyes turn as stormy as the afternoon had been the day before.

"He was." She wondered how much she should share. "It was my fault. I got kind of carried away."

"In that case...good. I don't feel like sharing you with the rest of the world yet." He stared out the window with his hands clasped behind his back. "Not until I have to."

"That's kind of ironic, isn't it?" She swallowed hard. "Unless you've changed your mind about our arrangement?"

Reed turned slowly to face her. He tipped his head to the side a bit. His stillness had never made her nervous before, but maybe his intensity had never been quite so focused on her. "Simon and Cooper aren't the rest of the world, they're part of mine. And we have you to thank for that. I never would have fallen into this kind of arrangement otherwise. It was you...and the damn frittata girl. I thought it would be enough to close my eyes and imagine she was you. Then I realized how much *more* there was to sex when I was sharing someone with those two. Bringing her three times the pleasure. It was incredible. Blew my mind. Then there was no going back."

She nodded weakly, twisting the hem of her shirt between her fingers.

"Are you changing your mind? It's okay if this is too much. I understand." Reed seemed resigned, as if he'd expected exactly that all along.

Andi couldn't deny that she was struggling this morning. She figured if she had any chance of surviving until graduation...and beyond...she had to be as honest as possible with him, despite the fact that she knew he wouldn't like what she had to say.

"That's just it—I'm not. I want this, Reed, even though I'm not sure it's best for you. I mean, I feel pretty slutty needing you as much as I do, considering that I've fucked both of your best friends in the past forty-eight hours." She couldn't meet his stare when she asked, "Are you *sure* that's not a problem for you?"

"What's not fucking okay with me is you demeaning yourself. Don't make me put you over my knee for saying shit like that." He would do it too, she didn't doubt it.

The purr that escaped was probably not the kind of encouragement she should have given him.

Reed strode to her and took hold of her shoulders. "I'm going to show you exactly how much it turns me on knowing that you've opened yourself to them. Finally learned to take. And then I'm going to let you see what it's like when I do the same for myself. Because once I let go of all this shit I've been keeping in check, it's not going to be...civilized."

Unlike Cooper, he wasn't gentle. Unlike Simon, he wasn't playful.

No, being with Reed was serious business.

Andi knew why he'd come to her last. He was capable of a whole new level of passion that he'd had the others build her up to. She hoped she was as ready as she was eager.

He wasn't the kind of guy to hedge his bets or take the long way around. "Be sure you're up for that."

"I am."

Reed was direct, and he was coming for her.

She couldn't wait to be caught.

CHAPTER TEN

eed captured Andi before she could utter any more reassurances. He backed her up against the kitchen wall, trapping her between it and the long, hard length of his torso. A squeak burst past her lips when she realized how much control he had over the situation.

Had always had over her.

"You've been planning this the whole week, haven't you?" she whispered.

The barest of sounds was all that was necessary since his lips hovered a hairsbreadth from hers.

"Much longer. I've been plotting this since the moment you applied for the open roommate spot on our lease." He was dead serious too. "I never thought I'd actually get to live out my fantasy."

"I want to be whatever you've dreamed of," she admitted.

"You are. Without trying, you're everything I could want. More than I need." He brushed his mouth over hers in a deceptively tender caress. She could feel his teeth behind his lips, though, waiting their turn to leave their mark.

"If I only get to do this once, with you…" A shiver made it hard to finish her thought, but he waited patiently to hear what she had to say. "I want it to be everything. I need that as much as you do. Don't half-ass this, Reed."

As if she'd unleashed a tiger, he growled and pounced. He crushed her with the well-muscled wall of his chest and jammed his thigh between her legs. While it held her up it also stoked the fire in her core, which grew from a glowing ember to something that could rage out of control and turn them both into a pile of ashes if they weren't careful.

It seemed the more she indulged sexually, the more insatiable she became. Good thing there were three of them and one of her. Soon she was going to be an unrepentant nymphomaniac, completely out of control and loving every second.

Or maybe desperation fueled her desire. Like a bear preparing for a barren winter, she had to hoard enough to get her through the cold, lonely nights ahead.

Either way, she couldn't seem to stop feasting on Reed, who didn't try to curb their shared appetite for desire.

She squirmed against him, trying to rub herself on him and glean what pleasure she could from his clenched quad against her mound. Meanwhile, she reached over and slid her hands beneath his shirt, running them up his back before raking her nails along either side of his spine.

Andi couldn't say what made her do it, except that she liked the idea of him bearing some proof of their time together. Unlike with Simon yesterday, he responded to her aggression by growing bolder himself. He wasn't the kind of man she'd ever be able to flip things around on. Instead, he would take her passion and match it. Escalate it.

As much as she'd enjoyed herself yesterday, today was a new day.

And she appreciated that about him.

No matter how brazen she got, how uninhibited, he wouldn't be fazed...or undermined.

Reed smiled down at her, though the expression held a steely edge more than kindness. "I like it when you're untamed. I always knew you had this in you, Andi. I'm glad you've realized it too, even if I only get a taste."

His fingers speared into her hair, fisting the strands until he held her face at precisely the angle he preferred for devouring her. When she moaned, close to begging for more already, he lifted her over his shoulder unceremoniously. With an arm banded just below her ass, he toted her into her room then tossed her onto the bed.

So different from how Cooper had treated her when he'd done nearly the same thing, yet with so much more finesse.

She didn't mind at all.

Having the best of both worlds...*three* worlds...was really the way to go.

The mounting anxiety in her about her pending departure made today's brand of loving more welcome. It gave her an outlet for her fear. It also allowed her to express the potency of her wish to cling to the things she loved about the present as she transitioned to her new life.

Raw and completely exposed, she allowed Reed to take her emotions and channel them into something constructive, something that would bring them both immense pleasure.

"That's it," he crooned as he stripped down with deliberate motions that unveiled his tattooed torso and the delicious lines that stretched from his hips to his groin. She'd spent hours staring at him working—shirtless—on her car, imaging exactly where they led. Now she knew, and it was far better than she'd imagined. She licked her lips as her gaze roamed over his fully erect cock. "You're going to give everything to me. All you have to worry about is pleasing me and letting me do the same for you. It's simple."

Andi swallowed and nodded. She could see the appeal of this flavor of intimacy.

For Reed, and for her, it would be a much needed release—a pressure valve that would allow them to operate logically in their day-to-day life without their brains overheating.

When he was nude and unflinchingly absorbing her gaze, as if completely sure of himself, he crossed to her closet and selected a few of her scarves before returning to the bed. Only then did he begin to remove her clothes too. He was careful not to rip or stretch them, but didn't waste any time with pleasantries either.

Soon enough, she was naked, lying before him.

She shifted, thinking of the beautiful women he was rumored to have partied with at Flesh. She knew now that he'd sealed the deal with every one of the dates he'd shared with Simon and Cooper. There was no denying his innate alpha could be persuasive.

"Don't you dare hide from me," he snapped.

Andi shivered. She allowed her arms to fall to her sides and her legs to spread the barest bit.

He took the scarves and trailed them over her, raising goose bumps in their wake as he studied each inch he teased, as though committing it to memory. "Every part of you is stunning to me, Andi. Your body, your laugh, your heart—all of it. Never doubt that."

When she merely stared up at him, transfixed, he asked, "Understand?"

"Yes, Reed."

"Good." He kissed her lightly then backed off far enough to ask. "Mind if I tie you up with these?"

"Yes. No. I mean, I definitely don't mind." She rolled her eyes at the jumble he'd already made of her ability to think clearly.

He laughed, though the sound was somewhat strained compared to usual. Before she could wonder if she'd made the right decision—and secure in the knowledge that if she hadn't, he'd release her immediately—he began to secure her to the brass bed.

"You have no idea how many times I imagined doing this since we picked this thing up from that estate sale." He groaned as he demonstrated his adeptness with knot work. Somehow she wasn't shocked in the least.

"I wish you had. I'm not blaming you—" she began, trying to make him comprehend.

"None of us were ready for something this serious. This real. Until it was almost too late." He glanced away then, only for a moment. "But now we are, and I'm not going to spend any more of our time regretting that it's not longer."

Andi nodded.

When he knelt by her shoulder to finish securing her second hand, she couldn't help but strain her neck toward him. With her tongue outstretched, she licked the head of his cock and sampled the drop of precome there.

"Is that really what you want?" he rasped.

She hummed and he took that as the encouragement it was.

Reed fed her his shaft, slowly, though she tried to swallow more of him than she was ready for. He backed off the moment she thought she might choke before easing inside once more. The transformation in his face from harsh to serene mesmerized her. Knowing she could do that for him made her never want to stop.

She swirled her tongue against the veins that increased in definition the more she experimented with different techniques. When she flicked a particularly sensitive spot just below the bulge of his head, he groaned then withdrew.

"As good as that feels, I'm not going to come before I'm finally buried in your tight cunt," he promised.

Hearing him talk like that to her exhilarated Andi. She squirmed, trying to press her thighs together to generate some friction. With her legs tied wide, it was no use.

He chuckled as he repositioned himself between them.

"You want that too?" he asked. "My dick stretching you as I fuck you so hard and deep that you can never forget what it's like to be mine, if only for today?"

"Yes!" She did. So badly.

"Then that's exactly what you're going to get." He slapped the fat tip of his cock against her clit several times. The shockwaves alone had her trembling all over. "Don't hold back, Andi. Remember?"

This time it was a sharper sensation when he used more pressure.

"Yes." It was the only word she could seem to say to him.

"Good. Because you're going to come for me now. Get yourself nice and wet inside so I can fuck you hard for as long as it takes to leave you boneless. By the time I'm done with you, you're going to think you'll never want to come again. And then I'm going to make you do it anyway."

Though his speech was enough to trigger her first orgasm, she didn't really think he could deliver on those wicked guarantees.

A few hours later, he'd rid her of every doubt.

Never once had he let go. Instead he'd edged himself, switching to eating her pussy when the urge to come nearly outstripped his willpower. It might have been more impressive to watch if she wasn't losing her mind to rapture on the regular.

"Mercy, Reed. Mercy," she panted after at least a dozen earth-shattering orgasms.

"That's all you had to say." He flashed a grin worthy of the Big Bad Wolf.

In a flash, he'd untied her and flipped her over. He placed her with her head on the mattress and her ass in the air, positioning her as if she were a poseable action figure, which she supposed she kind of was.

A giggle escaped her.

"You think this is funny, Andi?" He smacked her ass, sending shockwaves up her spine. Not bad ones, either. To her amazement, the sensations rekindled her lust.

"No. Please. Fuck me. Again." She reached for him and he made quick work of her arms, pulling them up and behind her before wrapping one of his big hands around both of her wrists to pin them in the small of her back.

"I think I will." He sank into her saturated pussy easily now. Still they both groaned at the reunion.

She was too busy enjoying his long strokes to realize quite what he was doing when he added a finger beside his cock.

That was, until he began to paint her natural lubrication over her back passage.

Andi bit the pillow beneath her as a whole host of new feelings bombarded her already overwhelmed senses. That went double when he pressed against her asshole and worked his digit inside. Never once did he stop fucking her while he did it, either.

"Tomorrow," he whispered into her ear, "this isn't going to be my finger."

The thought alone made her climax again, even harder. Her body wrung his cock and his finger at the same time. He took her to a place she'd never gone before. One where her pleasure kept exploding in burst after burst, an endless orgasm that he managed to prolong and sustain with his expert manipulation.

"Fuck, yes. Even hotter and tighter here," he groaned as he fucked her harder, deeper, faster.

It would be impossible for him *not* to come soon. He'd already surpassed her lofty expectations. It was the last thing she needed to feel completely satisfied with the journey he'd taken her on.

"Please, Reed," she begged. "Come. Come now. Tomorrow. There. No condom."

At first she wasn't sure he understood her broken ramblings.

Then she realized it was disbelief that had finally hitched his stride.

"Yeah?"

"Yes!" she screamed as another onslaught of pleasure wrung her pussy, and her ass followed suit. The combined vibrations, or her filthy promises, maybe both, finally broke his legendary restraint, taking him over the edge with her.

Reed roared as he shoved deep, locked entirely within her.

He anchored her against him as he spasmed, launching his come into the latex neither one of them wanted separating them again.

If she only got one more shot to show her roommates how much they mattered to her, she wanted it to count. Completely exhausted, both mind and body, she collapsed and remembered nothing more.

CHAPTER ELEVEN

Andi's life was starting to feel like some bizarre rendition of *Groundhog Day*.

She woke up alone again. Of course.

The only reminder that last night hadn't been a filthy dream was the slight discolorations that decorated her wrists and ankles.

It was like each of her roommates had given her a glimpse of what her future might be like three very different ways. If she committed to any one of them, she could be sickeningly happy.

Their generosity had taught her to be greedy, though. Trying all of them in a single bite, like some decadent version of Neapolitan ice cream, was sure to become her insta-favorite dessert.

If she was honest, she'd admit that some sliver of her had spent her time with each guy wondering about her other two roommates and what they were doing at those moments, or how they would feel if they could see what kind of naughty hijinks she was getting into courtesy of their buddy. Would they get off on watching her with their friends?

Would letting them do so amplify the already monumental pleasure they'd given her?

The ache between her legs said *hell yes*.

She hoped they didn't make her wait very long to find out the answer to her questions.

Adrenaline chased away any lingering grogginess. She bolted to the bathroom to take care of business, including a scorching shower, before wandering into their shared space.

An envelope made of fancy stationary with bits of flower petals in it caught her attention right away. She lifted it from the table and traced her finger over her name, written in Cooper's script on the front. When she got up the nerve to open it, carefully so she could save it for a premier spot in her scrapbook, she withdrew an elegant invitation from inside.

Congratulations!
Come celebrate with us.
After four years of hard work, now it's time to play. An afternoon of working up an appetite will be followed by dinner at Coeur. Wear your pretty purple dress for us…please.
Reed * Cooper * Simon

Her hands shook as she read the note. Not only because she'd drooled over classmates' photos from the swank restaurant forever, but also because she'd finally get to experience it with the only people who mattered to her.

Tomorrow she'd walk across the stage at graduation, accept her diploma, toss her cap, then close this chapter of her life. But tonight—they were right—was for celebrating their accomplishments. Including the very personal ones she'd made with the help of her roommates in the past few days.

Andi knew more about herself than she had thought possible.

She was prepared to go out into the world and...adult.

But somehow the thought didn't thrill her as much as it had previously.

A sniffle escaped as she ran her fingers over the trio of signatures on the invitation again and again.

"You can pick somewhere else if you don't like it," Simon startled her from her thoughts.

"Or wear anything you like." Reed glared at Cooper.

"Guys, it's the perfect going-away present. Thank you." She beamed at them, picking up the slack when their short-lived smiles faded at her uncouth reminder of their brief remaining time. Fortunately, she had an idea about how to lift their spirits. "And I think I have something you'll like too."

Without a single ounce of reluctance—they'd also gifted her with a newfound certainty of her allure—she lifted her shirt over her head and let it dangle from her index finger before allowing it flutter to the floor.

She wasn't wearing anything else.

Giving them the full view, she rotated slowly before sashaying into her bedroom.

Andi hadn't even made it to her bed before they were there, falling on her like a pack of wolves. Sexy wolves. Like maybe the werewolf variety. Because together they morphed into something downright beastly.

Reed nipped her breast while Cooper claimed her mouth and Simon sank to his knees to worship her ass. He was also the first to comment on her freshly shaven mound. "This is new."

She laughed into Cooper's mouth, sharing her joy with him. It'd only been two days, but she'd missed him and forgotten exactly how sensual his kisses were. Or maybe she hadn't had a point of reference until she'd taken the other guys for a test drive.

As prepared as she'd thought she was for this experience, Andi found herself awed as the three men worked together as a team. They played to their strengths and eliminated their weaknesses.

Cooper's polite seduction balanced Reed's rough touches, and Simon lightened both of their too-serious moods. All she had to do was be. They took care of the rest.

"Bring her to the bed," Reed commanded.

Without questioning him, Simon lifted her and placed her on the mattress. He climbed on with his shoulder resting on her headboard then pillowed her head on his thigh. His hand felt divine in her hair, stroking and soothing her jitters as Cooper joined them. He lay down so that his entire body pressed against hers from shoulders to her toes, which reached somewhere around his shins.

"Hey," he said by way of greeting before picking up where he had left off, kissing her.

Distracting her, she was sure, when she felt the bed dip once more and Reed spooned her from behind. His already stiff cock prodded her ass, reminding her of the promises he'd made the night before.

Sandwiched between the two guys, with Simon at her head, she might have felt claustrophobic. But she didn't. Not even a teensy bit.

"Still okay?" Cooper paused his kisses to wonder.

"Better by the second." She smiled up at Simon as she reached for his hand. Fishing around blindly, she found his shaft instead. That would work.

Andi massaged Simon with the same rhythm Cooper's tongue employed against her lips, gums and the roof of her mouth. Reed matched his tempo to the pace they set. All the while, the guys touched her. Everywhere they could reach was subject to their caresses.

The soft petting soothed her even as it aroused.

She'd never felt so safe or as cared for as she did between them.

That alone was enough to delight her. The physical aspect was pure bonus.

It didn't take too long for things to progress to the next level as Cooper guided her thigh over his hip. The motion positioned his cock at the apex of her legs. When Reed rocked his hips against her a little harder, he cursed and Cooper jerked. She figured their erections must have collided, given their proximity.

She knew they weren't bisexual. Still, the thought of them so close, teaming up to enhance her experience, made her even hotter.

Simon chuckled as he monitored the situation. He plumped in her fist, then groaned. "Better watch out, guys. I think she likes that a little too much."

By his reaction, she'd say he might also.

Andi winked at him and he seemed to flush.

Before she could instigate any additional shenanigans, Cooper drew her mind back to what he was doing. His cock prodded the entrance to her body and she called out his name.

"Right here." He kissed the tip of her nose when she tried to squirm closer.

"Inside," she demanded.

"Simon, toss me a condom?" he asked.

"No." She looked over her shoulder at Reed. "Didn't you tell them?"

He shook his head. "That's still what you want?"

"Yes. Please." Andi turned back to Cooper. "I'm on the Pill. Clean. Reed said you guys are too. I want you bare."

"Ah, shit." Simon lifted her head, angling it away from Cooper. He rubbed the tip of his cock over her lips and she licked him in welcome. "I was going to try to wait, to hold out, but…no way. Not if you're going there. I can't wait to see them fill you up."

In response, she opened her mouth and swallowed as much of his length as he fed her with every careful glide of his hips.

"Better catch up," Reed said to Cooper. "I have a feeling none of us are going to last as long as we'd like and I don't want to rush things back here."

A spark of anticipation married with nervousness tingled through her at that.

Would it hurt? Would she like it anyway?

Probably.

The rest of the week had proven that they had no difficulty pleasing her and she trusted that today would be no different. Unless it was better.

Cooper shifted, aiming his cock toward her pussy. But with one hand stuck beneath his side and the other clasping her thigh to keep her open, he kept slipping across her instead of boring inside.

"Need a hand?" Reed asked.

"Do it." Cooper gave his permission.

The grunt that shook Cooper's chest, and her breasts at the same time, made it clear he didn't care who was touching him, so long as it meant the pressure on his shaft increased. Andi wished she could have seen Reed's fingers wrapped around his friend like that.

It would be fodder for her masturbation sessions for years to come, she was sure.

Then he was there, pressing into her, filling her with warmth and firmness. Giving her something to hold within her and keeping her undulating muscles busy with something to work. Andi sucked Simon harder, loving the feel of one of them at each end of her. She felt stuffed with life and love and pleasure.

And cock.

Andi laughed to herself at that, nearly choking on Simon in the process.

"What the hell is so funny?" he wondered.

"Tell you later," she said, then got back to work.

Reed growled before raking his teeth down the nape of her neck. "I think I should give you something to get serious about."

She shuddered, a pulse of bliss wringing her and causing her to clench on Cooper.

"Fuck yes, Reed. She wants it," he said.

"I know she does." He began to massage her ass, working inward until his fingers danced over her hole. "Distract her while I do this right."

The next several minutes passed in a blur as Cooper fucked her with artful glides that left her oblivious to any prickles of pain Reed caused as he worked her open with a finger, then two or three. Simon had to take a break, so she switched to suckling his balls. She loved watching his toes curl when she traced the center seam of his sac with the tip of her tongue.

When, finally, Cooper sank deep into her and held still, Reed was right there to take her higher.

He fit his lubed cock to her ass and sank in bit by bit, making her cry out around Simon.

It burned at first. She wasn't going to lie about that. Still buried to the root, Cooper relaxed her with gentle nuzzles and soft strings of nonsense whispered into her ear.

As her body adjusted to Reed's girth, the stinging began to morph from pain into something distinctly *not* pain. It was an extreme sensation, one that heightened the rest of the intersections of her guys' skin with hers. She felt every place they touched acutely.

Even her tongue on Simon's shaft seemed more alive.

Andi felt as though she had superhuman powers. Doubly so when she saw, and heard, the impact she had on these three spectacular men.

They rode her together, working collectively or in counterpoint but never at random. Everything they did to her was deliberate and well-orchestrated by Reed. She saw how each of their personalities entwined to create the perfect lover for her.

That thought alone was enough to have her hovering on the verge of what promised to be the greatest orgasm of all time.

Reed, so in tune with her and her body, put the others on alert. The instant she was ready, they were right there with her. "We're going over together. Now."

Cooper ground against her, increasing the friction across her clit. She couldn't have stopped herself even if she'd wanted to. The first hot wash of Reed's come in her ass made her peak with him. And the clamping of her pussy around Cooper did the same for him. Simon squeezed her fingers and tried to withdraw from between her lips.

She refused to let him escape her throat.

Instead, she hummed at the first splash of his seed on her tongue then began to swallow every drop that pulsed from his cock. If she could only do this once, she didn't want to waste a damn thing. Bruising fingers gripped her hips and shoulders as her roommates clung to her like a life raft in a turbulent ocean.

When they could do more than simply endure the blasts of gale-force passion they'd whipped up together, Simon was the first to break the quiet.

"That looked...amazing," he sighed, his voice full of wonderment.

Andi pressed a kiss beside his half-hard cock and masterminded a devious plan on the fly.

"Why don't you let me suck you until you're ready again? We'll swap positions. No reason you should miss out on the good stuff." She grinned up at Simon, who blinked then nodded furiously.

"You're sure?" Reed hesitated. The other guys waited for her to confirm.

"If you try to stop me, I'll knee you in the balls." Andi grinned as he reflexively covered his junk.

"Give the lady what she wants," he instructed. And they did.

They tried it again, and again, just to be sure every possible combination was equally as marvelous, until she believed she might know how it felt to be an amusement park ride—spun around and ridden endlessly. She loved every moment.

At some point, she lost track of what went where and who was doing those magical things to her each part of her body. The three guys melded into one. Where she went and whoever they were with after this didn't matter. She would be forever theirs.

Her mind detached from her physical being, ensuring all she could do was feel and react accordingly.

Utter decadence.

The guys didn't seem to have any complaints either.

A long, long while later they lay wrecked, finally spent.

Andi snuggled among them, replete and drifting for some undetermined amount of time. She figured it was the utter relaxation of her body and the endorphins flooding her brain that made her speak her errant thoughts out loud. "What if there's a way to make this work long distance?"

It was as if she went from being nestled in a pile of puppies to lying among tombstones for how stiff the guys went. Reed especially. A mask dropped over his face, cutting her off from every genuine feeling he'd exposed previously.

"We've already brainstormed every possible solution," he explained. "It won't work."

"Why not?" She swallowed. "I mean, I know I'll be four hours away, but we could visit on weekends and holidays. The time in between would suck..."

Shaking her head, she stopped her wishful thinking. "It's not fair to you guys to ask you to give up a real relationship for me. I'm sorry."

Cooper surprised her by taking her hand. "Think about what you're saying. You'd be alone most of the time. Waiting around for one of us to show up. And how would you...pick? Or maybe you know which of us you'd prefer to be with after the past week?"

"Are we on the same planet?" She rose, tugging on her clothes as she spun to face them. She couldn't bear to be so naked. "Why couldn't I have you all to myself?"

And when she said it like that...it seemed awfully selfish. How could she be enough for the three of them? Not for a fun night of fucking, but for something more permanent?

She couldn't, she supposed.

Jumbled emotions had her pacing, mumbling to herself.

Simon hopped off the bed and crossed to her. He hugged her tight then said, "Andi, this is fun. And amazing. But what are you going to do when there's a Halloween party at your new boss's house? Or a fundraiser? Take three guys with you everywhere? Rotate us? Make one of us your public guy, and the other two your sidepieces?"

"I..." She shrugged helplessly. How could she hurt them like that?

"You haven't had time to really digest this." Reed stayed put. "We have. We've thought about it a lot."

They obviously didn't like the verdict they'd reached any more than she did, but what other choice did the four of them have? She could see it their way when she thought about how unfair it would be to them.

Cooper glowered. "I can see in your face that you still don't get it."

"We're not worried about us." Reed shook his head as he continued, "People will talk. They won't necessarily be kind to someone who's chosen an alternative lifestyle. And we won't be anywhere around to protect you if you need us. We won't put you in that kind of danger. Shit, look what almost happened last weekend! No more chances like that. If some wacko hurt you..."

Simon moaned.

"Okay, fine." She rubbed her temples then said the unimaginable. "I won't take the job. I'll stay. Here...with you."

"No!" they shouted together.

As much as she wished they were wrong, they weren't.

If she didn't go, she would regret it for the rest of her life. Everything she'd worked for would be for nothing. Her heart broke into a million tiny pieces. Sacrificing one dream for another wasn't easy. It gored her so damn bad that she reacted like any wounded animal would.

Andi didn't waste any time after that. Staying longer would prolong the torture.

She ignored their protests—refusing their help—and immediately began hauling her stuff out of her room. One box at a time, she packed up every bit of her existence and erased it from their apartment. It didn't take as long as she might have thought. With that finished, she went to the bathroom, blew her nose, then took one final look around the kitchen before enclosing the doorknob in her fingers, willing her wrist to turn.

"Andi, where are you going?" Reed tried to grab her, but she shrugged out of his hold. "It'll be dark before you get to Cunningham. Late. You've got to be worn out after today. This week. Don't do this. We'll leave if you want. It's not safe for you to drive so upset!"

"That's not your concern," she snapped.

"You'll always be—"

"No, I won't. As of right now, I'm not. Not anymore." She barely choked back a sob. "Now move!"

It took Cooper and Simon tag teaming Reed to drag him back, giving her the chance to escape.

"You're going to miss graduation? Our celebration dinner?" He simmered down at that. "Not after how hard you've worked. Don't go, Andi. Not yet."

"It's time." She swallowed the knot in her throat as she tried to be strong enough for all of them.

Andi looked at each of the three special men who had made her college years full and rich. She'd never forget their time together or the spectacular way they'd ended it. "I love you. Goodbye."

She wasn't proud of it, but she turned and ran while she could.

The rush of blood through her system made it impossible to hear what they called after her. Tears poured down her cheeks as she drove away, refusing to so much as glance in the rearview mirror.

Forward.

She was moving ahead.

Getting on with the rest of her life, having far more experience than she'd bargained for.

CHAPTER TWELVE

One month later

Andi sat on her couch, staring at the ginormous flat screen she'd bought with her first real paycheck. Whatever show was on, she hadn't seen a second of it. It droned, providing background noise. She hadn't realized how damn quiet an apartment could be.

Her financial conservatism had insisted she put enough in savings to cover next month's rent on her bright, cheery apartment, which felt like an extravagance since it was larger than the space she'd shared with three roommates. Another chunk of change had gone toward a certified pre-owned car that didn't leak oil. Then she'd written checks for her first student loan payments, bought groceries for a month, started a rainy day fund, and she'd still had some room to spare in her budget.

It felt fucking weird.

So she'd splurged on the TV. Yet, somehow, she already could tell she wouldn't be using it much. It just wasn't the same without the clean but battered blue couch and the three guys who had overcrowded it in her last home.

A knock on the door startled her from her trance.

At first she planned to ignore it. She didn't know anyone here, so it could only be a solicitor or maybe a group of church people hoping to save her soul. When it came again, louder this time, she changed her mind. After all, she hadn't talked to anyone outside of the fellow employees she met at her new job. They were nice enough, but they weren't friends.

Yes, she was turning into *that* person. Next she'd be making small talk in the frozen food aisle at the QuickPick so she didn't lose her damn mind.

It might be too late for that.

Annoyed with herself, she marched to the door and flung it open.

"Hey."

The last person she expected to see was the guy standing there. Simon.

Well, okay, maybe the *very* last person she'd expect to see was Reed. He was too stubborn to cave like that. He was the only one of her three ex-roommates who hadn't emailed her in the past month. Not that she'd responded to the other two. She didn't know what to say and didn't trust her fingers not to type things she shouldn't admit. Like an addict, she'd had to quit them cold turkey.

Withdrawal was a bitch.

One look at Simon and she knew she'd be hooked again after a single hit.

"What are you doing here?" She tamped down the urge to fly into his arms and smother him with a desperate mega-hug.

"Does that mean you won't give me a tour of your new place?" he asked. "Seems like a huge step up. I understand if you want to keep the riffraff out."

"Shit, sorry." She chewed her lip as she debated whether or not it was wise. It wasn't. But she did it anyway. "Come in."

He nodded and whistled softly as he took in her new surroundings.

"Thanks," she said with a hint pride. Her hard work *had* paid off.

"Anyway, uh...this came for you today." Simon held up a thick envelope with DO NOT BEND stamped all over it in red block letters. "I thought you might like to have your diploma. Since you missed graduation."

His wince made it clear that he understood how big of a sacrifice that had been for her.

"So you hopped in your car and drove four hours to bring it to me?" Her eyes went wide as she accepted the package.

"Yeah, well, I'm not really big on planning, you know?" He shrugged. "Didn't have anything better to do."

"What's really going on?" She noticed the way he shifted his weight from foot to foot. Nervous, so unlike him.

"There's something I want to tell you." He swallowed hard.

"What's wrong?" She put her hands on his shoulders, fighting the paranoid pessimism that she'd picked up right around the time her second parent had broken the news to her that he had a terminal illness. "Is someone sick? Hurt? Worse? Tell me straight. You're scaring me."

"Shit. It's nothing like that." Simon sighed then invaded her living room as if he belonged there. When he plopped onto her couch, she instantly liked it better.

"Then what?" She sat beside him and took his hand.

"I know a guy..." He trailed off then started again. "Okay, no. That's bullshit. A friend of mine has a friend who plays for the Sabertooths. I called in a favor. He put me in touch with the head of the training staff. It turns out they can use a guy like me. The job is mine if I want it."

"They play here, in Cunningham?" Her jaw dropped.

"Yeah. I mean, I'd have to travel with the team during the season, but most of the time..."

"Wow. That's—" Andi shook so hard, still trying to digest his revelation and what that could mean for them, that when another knock came at the door, she literally could not stand to answer it.

"Hang out a second. Take some deep breaths. I'll get rid of whoever this is, and we'll talk more." He stroked her hair. "You don't have to decide right now. I thought I should tell you in person.

No pressure. But I'm not going to leave until you're settled down, okay?"

She nodded as she chewed her nails, a bad habit she'd picked up lately.

When Simon opened the door, she certainly wasn't prepared for him to shout, "What the hell?"

Her gaze whipped up and saw Cooper standing there, equally as confused, on the other side of the door.

"I could say the same." He glared at Simon.

"I didn't break our pact. I just... Something came up and I wanted to talk to her about it before I said anything to you guys. Look, it was a dumb idea—"

Andi didn't like the sound of that.

"Wait. No, it wasn't, Simon." She tried to rise. Her shaking legs pitched her right back onto the couch.

Both of the guys were beside her in an instant. Cooper knelt, then took her hand. "God, I've missed you, Andi. But...are you okay? Do you want me to go? I'll kick him out too."

She shook her head. Now that they were here, she couldn't stand to think of them leaving. Especially not after the bomb Simon had dropped. How would Cooper take the news?

She shouldn't have worried.

He destroyed more of the carefully crafted vision she'd built for how her life would go from here on out when he cleared his throat. "I have some news too."

Her gaze snapped to his.

"I transferred to the law program at U of C. I was wondering if I could crash with you for a while, until I get my own place. It happened kind of fast. Classes for their summer semester start on Monday."

"What?" she and Simon asked simultaneously, with equal amounts of shock coloring their question.

"I'm not expecting anything. You know...between us. That's not what I'm asking. I thought—" Before Cooper could finish explaining exactly what he had imagined, the door nearly rattled off its hinges. This time it wasn't a knock that intruded on their conversation, but a series of bangs that could only belong to one person.

"Oh shit." Simon's eyes went wide and he jogged to answer that nonverbal demand before her pretty white door got smashed to smithereens.

He was smart enough to duck as it opened, barely dodging Reed's punch. Holding his hands up, he said, "Hey, you're here too. Don't get pissed that we beat you to it."

"*I* was only planning to drive past and check out the neighborhood when I saw both of your cars sitting out at the curb. What the fuck?" Reed roared as he stomped into the living room.

Suddenly it seemed a lot smaller than it had before.

Andi cut through their testosterone-laden crap with the swipe of a hand. "What were you doing spying on me, Reed? How many times have you gone by and not had the balls to say hello?"

He scrubbed his hand over his mouth before admitting, "A few."

"Now *that's* pathetic," Cooper said before thinking better of it. "At least when I drive four fucking hours to see a woman, I come inside."

"I was here on business," Reed shouted.

"What do you mean?" she wondered.

"The investors I brought on own a property out here. It's got the facilities I need to get things up and running. And since it's already part of their portfolio, they're willing to lease it to me at a substantial discount in exchange for a portion of future profits." He sighed. "It's been in the works for a while, but I didn't want to say anything—"

"Until you knew for sure." An enormous grin broke over her face as she finished his thought.

Could this really be happening?

Simon joined her, since he had all the pieces too.

"Well, guys, there's one thing I know for certain already." She choked on the admission. "I've missed every one of you like hell. And...I love you. Each of you for who you are separately and I'm extra in love with you for what you're like together. We have something that works between us. Hell, we've practically been in a damn relationship for the past four years, just without sex. What fun is that?"

Actually, it had been amazing. And it could only get better.

She continued, "I know we still have a lot to work on. The other issues you guys raised about turning this relationship into a forever thing are still going to be hurdles we have to clear. But I'm willing to figure it out if you are. What do you say?"

"I say I love you too, Andi. I don't care how we have to do it, but I'm committed to making it work." Reed charged to her and swooped her into his arms. He kissed her until she was dizzy before handing her off to Cooper, then Simon, who convinced her they felt the same way without having to say a single word.

"So I only have one question then…" Simon said with a smirk when he had taken his fill. "How big is your bed?"

"Pretty sure we're going to need a new one." She laughed then, thinking of the four of them jammed onto the queen-sized mattress, which had seemed enormous—and empty—the night before.

"Damn straight. And I hope you don't have plans for the rest of the weekend. We're not leaving this house until you remember what it's like to belong to us," Reed swore.

"Sounds good. Besides, it's been a bitch having to do my own laundry, cook, pay bills, and take care of my car. I'm spoiled and I like it that way." She couldn't say that without cracking a smile. Though she'd only been teasing, they didn't seem to mind.

"You haven't seen anything yet," Cooper promised right before he kissed the shit out of her. The happiness that fizzed through her veins eclipsed anything she'd felt before, proving his point quite nicely.

"You know, that sounded kind of sexist, Andi. Not like you..." Reed lectured with an evil twist to the corner of his lips.

"I *am* a bad girl now. Maybe you should spank me for it."

"Maybe I should." He stalked closer with a growl that didn't scare her in the least. But she shrieked and let him chase her around their new home—any place they were together would deserve that title—for a little while before getting caught.

After all, anticipation made things so much sweeter.

She knew that from experience.

to the lust that's been arcing between them since day one. In the aftermath of the best sex of her life, she whispers her most secret desire: to be ravaged by his crew.

She never expected Mike would dare her to take what she wants—or that the freedom to make her most decadent desires come true could be the foundation for something lasting...

Warning: This book may cause you to spontaneously combust as five hot guys bring a woman's wildest fantasies to life during one blazing summer affair.

EXCERPT FROM KATE'S CREW, POWERTOOLS BOOK 1

Kate wiped her palms on her paint-splattered cutoffs before adjusting her grip on the rebuilt window casement. A flash of tan skin drew her attention to glistening muscles. They rippled over five sexy frames as the crew renovating the townhouse next door hammered nail after nail into their first-story roof, just a few feet below her perch.

From inside the bedroom where she worked, she inched to the edge of the ladder rung then craned her neck through the opening in front of her for a glimpse of the intricate tattoo spanning Mike's broad shoulders. Instead, she caught him reaching up to their stash of supplies for another pack of shingles. When her gaze latched onto the drop of sweat that slid along his neck, she forgot to breathe. She watched in fascination as it journeyed over his defined pecs and six-pack abs. After it was absorbed in the ultra-low-riding jeans snugged to his trim hips by a bulging tool belt, she heaved a sigh of relief.

Kate swiped at a blob of paint that had plopped onto her wrist unnoticed while she'd ogled Mike. Her tongue moistened her lips as she imagined licking a similar trail down his body. The edge of the fresh trim gouged her thigh as she strained for a better view. The gasp she made busted her. His head lifted, catching her spying. Great, now she'd never convince him to take it easy with his persistent innuendo or date invites. And, no matter how much she wanted to, she couldn't indulge either of their desires.

Mike threw her a dazzling victory grin. The anticipation sparkling in his cocky stare blasted a shockwave through her, screwing with her balance. The ladder wobbled then tipped. She probably could have righted herself if she hadn't been standing on tiptoes to maximize her view of the scenery. In slow motion, she watched his expression morph from flirtatious to horrified.

Kate flung out her arms in an attempt to catch the frame before she tumbled through it but the momentum swung her around. Her temple grazed the custom-made pewter latch she'd installed the day before. She hung, suspended in midair, as Mike rose from his crouch. The other guys began to turn toward her, but he was already sprinting for the edge.

Terror froze her insides when he launched himself across the ten-foot gap between their houses. Then she spun away, losing sight of him. She braced for imminent impact.

Shit, this is going to hurt.

Everything happened at once. Air whooshed from her lungs when she slammed, on her side, onto the roof. She rolled, flexing her ankles in an attempt to find purchase that would halt her skid toward the brink. But her knee wrenched at an awkward angle while she continued to rake over the slate. Her hand caught the ridge of an attic vent, slowing her descent, but gravity overcame the tenuous hold. Her frantic fingers recoiled from the sharp metal edge.

The gutters rushed closer, her last hope. After that, she'd have to pray the evergreen shrubs would cushion her, preventing any broken bones. The heels of her work boots hit the aluminum edging but kept going. Her legs dangled in thin air.

Then a strong hand banded around her wrist. Her arm nearly jerked from the socket as she lurched to a stop. Kate shoved on the edging shingles with her free hand, fighting to stay on the roof.

"Son of a bitch!" Mike hauled her the rest of the way up.

ABOUT THE AUTHOR

Jayne Rylon is a *New York Times* and *USA Today* bestselling author. She received the 2011 RomanticTimes Reviewers' Choice Award for Best Indie Erotic Romance.

Her stories used to begin as daydreams in seemingly endless business meetings, but now she is a full-time author, who employs the skills she learned from her straight-laced corporate existence in the business of writing. She lives in Ohio with two cats and her husband, the infamous Mr. Rylon.

When she can escape her purple office, Jayne loves to travel the world, SCUBA dive, take pictures, avoid speeding tickets in her beloved Sky and—of course—read.